The Cats That Surfed the Web

Karen Anne Golden

Copyright

This book or eBook is a work of fiction. Names, characters, places and incidents are products of the author's imagination or are used fictitiously. Any resemblance to actual events, locales, persons or cats, living or dead, is entirely coincidental.

Edited by Vicki Braun

Cover design by Christy Carlyle of Gilded Heart Design

ISBN-13: 978-1494253240
ISBN-10: 1494253240

Dedication

For Dad

Table of Contents

Prologue

The driver jammed on the brakes of his rental car in front of the pink mansion on Lincoln Street. "This can't be it," he said incredulously, shocked by the massive size of the three-story Victorian house.

A few minutes earlier he had left the town's hotel and restaurant, then tapped an address into his GPS. The feminine voice had told him to take a wrong turn and he'd almost driven into the Wabash River. Now, even more annoyed at being in this hick town with only two stop lights, he double-checked the address. The brass house numbers above the columned veranda matched, so he backed up the car, turned into the snow-covered driveway, and parked behind an older model Toyota with New York plates.

As he wrestled on his coat, he climbed out of the driver's seat, wincing at a sudden, searing pain that began in his right side. A blast of cold Indiana air penetrated his coat, making him focus on the task at hand. As he looked through the arches of the covered carport, he saw a figure wearing a hooded parka dart from the far end of the driveway, out-of-sight behind the corner of the house. He thought it was his ex-girlfriend, Katherine, who was the

1

main reason for his surprise visit. "Katherine," he yelled. "Katz, is that you, honey?" he asked in a charming voice.

Trudging to the back of the house, he called out her name again. The back door was slightly ajar, so he pushed it open and stepped down several steps into a windowed sunroom. Stamping his boots on the welcome mat, he cried out as the pain returned. Holding onto his side, he found another door that led to a mechanical room; it was illuminated by a florescent bulb, which flickered on and off with a loud buzz.

He heard footsteps back in the dark basement.

"Stop playing games," he shouted. "I know you're here, Katz. I really need to talk to you." Motionless he stood, held his breath, and listened. He heard no answer or further movement.

Now he was getting angry. And the pain just wouldn't go away. *What the hell is happening to me?* he thought. "Look, give me a break. It was a nightmare getting out here. My flight from LaGuardia was delayed. I was supposed to fly into Indianapolis, but we were re-routed to Chicago. The car rental place was a zoo. The drive down here to Hicksville was the worst."

Something fell to the floor, and he thought he heard a hissing sound. Heading toward the noise, he stumbled into a small room with thick stone walls. The room was dimly lit by a frosted glass window, set high above the floor. His eyes quickly adjusted to the semi-darkness. He could make out the vague shape of someone standing in the corner.

"Why are you acting so freaking weird?" he asked, teetering forward.

An eerie shaft of light shone through the window, revealing a tall, svelte Siamese cat with its back arched like a Halloween cat. It began to sway from side-to-side in some kind of strange dance. The cat's eyes were red and almost seemed to glow. It murmured a low, menacing growl.

The man turned to the stranger. "Who are you?" he asked. His own words rang painfully in his ears as a shadow fell across the room.

The figure in the parka emerged from the darkness, holding a knife in one hand and a rusty-brown cat in the other. The cat struggled to be free.

"Put the knife down," the man demanded. "No one needs to be hurt here."

The hooded figure threw the cat at him.

When he put his arms up to catch the cat, the stranger stabbed him in his left side, high under his armpit. A sharp pain ripped through his chest and he gasped for air. He stumbled backward, then fell to the floor. The rusty-brown cat hissed, then ran to the corner and collapsed on her side.

The Siamese shrieked and lunged at the assailant. She dug her claws into the parka, pulling the hood down and drawing blood from the head. The attacker dislodged the Siamese, then leaned over the man's body and inserted a gold object in his mouth. The Siamese quickly got back on all fours and chased the assailant out of the room. When the cat returned, she circled the body once, wildly sniffing the air with her fangs bared. She began to wail a shrill, mournful cry.

Chapter One

Katherine Kendall struggled with a stack of instruction manuals and a laptop computer case as she jostled her way along the crowded sidewalk on Fifth Avenue. Reaching her office building, she leaned into the revolving door and was nearly whisked away by the same bicycle-riding messenger who had almost flattened her in the middle of Madison Avenue. Katherine stumbled forward and fell on one knee. The laptop case went sailing through the air and skidded to a dead stop fifteen feet away. The manuals scattered across the highly polished marble floor.

"Well, *excuse* me," the woman said sarcastically to the perpetrator in blue biker's tights.

The messenger darted to the right to avoid tripping over her and said, "You again!" Dashing to the first elevator bank, he hurtled into the crowded elevator as its doors closed.

The Colombian doorman started to run after the biker, but was too late. He went over to the woman to offer assistance. "Are you okay?"

"I've been better," she said, getting up. She rubbed her knee through the large tear in her new suit pants. "I hope my computer is okay."

The doorman retrieved the laptop and handed it to her. "I think it's all right, being in a padded case and all."

"Thanks, Fernando," she said, leaning over to pick up the manuals.

"Here, let me do that," he said, collecting the remaining booklets and stacking them on her computer. "Want me to help you to the eighteenth floor?"

"No, that's fine, but thanks for offering," she said. Attempting a smile, she walked to the elevator bank. She pressed the button with her chin, then waited a few seconds for the next elevator. When an elevator opened, she slipped inside and tried to press the floor number with her nose.

A smartly dressed businessman hurried behind her and said, "What floor?"

"Eighteen," she answered.

He pressed two buttons: eighteen and twenty-three. He smiled and stood back in the corner. "I'll be on the lookout for the messenger from Hell," he said with a wink.

"I wish hail the size of golf balls to fall on his head," she muttered.

"And a flat tire in the middle of Fifth Avenue," the businessman added.

The doors swished open and she walked into an expensively decorated receiving area. Striding past the receptionist, Katherine rounded the corner and headed for her cubicle, which was down the hall.

The receptionist called after her, "Ms. Kendall, I have a message for you here at the front desk."

"One second," Katherine answered. She deposited the heavy burden on her desk, then walked back to the receptionist. "Rosemary, this is a computer company. We want you to get used to sending and receiving email," she explained. "Please email short phone messages from your computer. Anything longer, just forward the message to my voice mail."

Rosemary was in her mid-seventies, with ramrod posture and patrician bearing. She was from the old school of reception and loved to write on pink slips of paper. "An attorney from Indiana telephoned and said that he urgently needs to speak to you." She handed Katherine a pink message slip.

"Mark Dunn," Katherine read out loud. "In reference to Orvenia Colfax." She looked up from the message slip. "He didn't leave a number?"

"He said he'd call you back," the receptionist added.

"Great Aunt Orvenia," Katherine said curiously. "I wonder what this is all about?"

The phone rang on the receptionist's PBX board. "Computer Net. How may I direct your call?" Rosemary answered cheerily. "Oh yes, Sir. She just returned. Hold on, please." To Katherine she mouthed the words, "It's him again."

"Put it through to my line, Rosemary. Thanks," she said, as she rushed back to her desk and answered the call. "Katherine Kendall."

"Hello, Ms. Kendall. My name is Mark Dunn. I'm a lawyer in Erie, Indiana. I represent your Great Aunt Orvenia's estate."

"Estate?" Katherine said uncertainly. "Is my great aunt trying to get a hold of me?"

"I've been trying to reach you, but we had little to go on except that you live in New York."

"So how did you find me?" she asked warily.

"I did various online searches, but found out where you worked on your *Facebook* page—"

"What can I do for you?" she asked abruptly, cutting him off.

"I hate to be the bearer of bad news," he said, pausing for a moment, "but your great aunt passed away several weeks ago."

"Oh, no."

"I'm sorry," he said.

"What happened?"

"Massive coronary. She died very peacefully," he said. "Ms. Kendall, the reason I'm calling is that I'm handling your great aunt's estate. Over the past year she had me draft several versions of her will, but several months ago, she listed you as her most significant residuary beneficiary."

"Me?" Katherine asked dubiously. "I never met the woman. Why would she list me as a . . . excuse me . . . what's a residuary beneficiary?"

"It means that you're the sole heir to receive the bulk of your great aunt's estate, provided you abide by one condition—"

"Condition?" she interrupted.

"In order to receive monies from the estate, you must reside in her house and take care of her cat for one year—"

"Take care of a cat," Katherine said skeptically.

"Yes, a cat," he repeated. "In one year, you'll have full control of your residuary legacy—the money—and can dispose of the property in any manner you see fit. However, during the first year you'll receive thirty thousand dollars immediately, plus seventy thousand at the end of six months' time. Provided you take good care of the cat, you'll receive full use of your great aunt's house, plus the rest of your money at the end of the year. The estate will pay the utilities, insurance and property taxes so long as the estate is open."

"One hundred thousand dollars," Katherine repeated in disbelief. "Money, a house, and a cat! I find this very difficult to believe. And by the way, one of the few things I specifically remember about my great aunt from my mom is that she was allergic to cats."

"Apparently not too allergic," he said. "Two years ago, she bought an Abyssinian female from a breeder in Wisconsin. I personally drove her up there to pick up the kitten."

"I already have my hands full with three Siamese," she said, still in shock. "Two seal-points and one lilac-point," she added quickly.

"What's one more?" the attorney joked.

"Where's the cat now?" Katherine asked with sudden interest.

"She's staying at a local veterinarian's office. Orvenia provided that the cat be boarded for no longer than ninety days. I'm hoping that we can get her back home as soon as possible after you move."

"Move? You want me to move where?"

"Erie, Indiana."

"Into my great aunt's house? I just signed a two-year lease on my apartment in Manhattan."

"I'm sorry, Ms. Kendall, we can't wait that long. I might be able to get you out of your lease. I have a colleague who's an attorney in New York," he explained. "Have you ever seen your great aunt's house?" he asked.

"No," she answered. "I've never even been to the state of Indiana."

"Orvenia was a very wealthy lady and lived in a mansion built in 1897. The house has three floors and seventeen rooms."

"Seventeen rooms!" she said aghast. "Listen, Mr. Dunn. This is too much to absorb in one phone call."

"Please call me 'Mark,'" he said amicably.

"Only if you stop calling me 'Ms. Kendall.' My name is Katherine," she replied.

"Okay, Katherine, I need an answer soon," he urged. "The cat is currently being boarded at the vet's office, in a cage, which isn't the ideal place to keep an energetic pet," he reminded.

"What's the cat's name? You keep referring to her as the cat."

"Her name is Abigail," he said. "Orvenia thought it would be a good name for an Abyssinian."

I wonder how my Siamese would get along with her, she thought. "What happens to the estate when Abigail dies?"

"The will specifies that when the cat—I'm sorry—when Abigail dies, she's to be cremated and placed in your great aunt's burial crypt."

"Orvenia must have adored that cat," Katherine said.

"But after you've cared for Abigail for one full year, you'll receive the rest of the residuary legacy, which consists of full legal title to the house, plus securities currently valued at . . ." he hesitated, then said, "Forty-four million."

"Forty-four million dollars!" she shouted over the phone. "Are you serious? My great aunt, who I've never met, left me forty-four million dollars?"

"Remember, the will made that gift conditional," the attorney said.

"Okay, what happens if I don't accept the terms?"

"In that case I must hire full-time, live-in help to take care of the animal. This person would receive the hundred thousand dollars that would otherwise go to you, plus full use of the house. And because you wouldn't be entitled to the forty-four million, sixty percent of it would go to the town of Erie, ten percent to the County Animal Welfare Society, and thirty percent would be added to a trust set up for the benefit of your great aunt's housekeeper."

"Mr. Dunn, I mean Mark . . . I'm late for a training class I'm teaching. This is very complicated and bewildering. I must have time to gather my thoughts. Is there any way you can email me the provisions of the will?"

"Certainly. What's the address?"

Katherine gave it to him, as well as her cell phone number. "If you can't reach me on my cell, here's my home number."

"Expect an email within the hour," he said.

"If you try to reach me at home and you keep getting a busy signal, text me and I'll call you right back. Sometimes one of my cats kicks the receiver off the hook."

Mark laughed. "Your cat answers the phone?"

"Scout, my cat, that is, used to belong to a magician who used her in his act. One of her tricks was to answer a telephone, but that has nothing to do with this conversation."

Mark said seriously, "Perhaps you'll tell me the rest of that story someday. It's been very nice speaking to you, Katherine, but I need an answer from you as soon as possible."

"Thanks for calling," she said, hanging up the phone.

She immediately sent a text message to her best friend, Colleen. With thumbs flying, she keyed in, "Can you meet me after work at that wine and cheese place on 53rd Street? I have news that will blow you away."

* * * *

"I got here as soon as I could," Colleen said, darting to the table. Her long red hair was wind-blown and matted against her face. "My boss gave me this last-minute project and insisted I finish before I left. How long have you been waiting?" she asked, taking her coat off and throwing it over a chair.

"Not long. Just a few minutes," Katherine answered.

"So, what's the news? A love interest, perhaps?" Colleen asked mischievously.

"Oh, please," Katherine said, slightly annoyed. "Sit down and brace yourself."

The waiter came over and said to Colleen, "What will it be?"

"Bring me a Guinness," she said.

"Draught or bottle?" he asked.

"Bottle."

He looked at Katherine.

"I'm still nursing my Cabernet. Please bring us some Boursin and Carr crackers."

He nodded and headed to the bar.

"What is it, Katz?" Colleen asked, slightly out-of-breath. "You're as pale as a ghost."

"What would you do if you received word that an elderly great aunt who you've never met left you her house, money and property?"

"Oh, no way," Colleen said dismissively. "I have three aunts back in Ireland, and if I'm lucky they'll leave me their sacred recipe for Irish Soda Bread."

"My great aunt in Indiana passed away several weeks ago and left me everything."

"I'm sorry to hear that, Katz. Why didn't you ever mention her?"

"She was my mother's aunt, and became the black sheep of the family when she ran off to the Midwest to marry an older man."

"Why would that make her a black sheep?"

Katherine shrugged, "I don't know. My mom rarely talked about her. Anyway, my great aunt's attorney called today and said she'd left me—"

"How much are we talking about here?" Colleen interrupted.

"An incredible amount of money," Katherine said. She leaned in and whispered, "Forty-four million dollars!"

Colleen's mouth dropped open. "You can't be serious," she said, then added, "I'd take the money and run."

"But there's a condition," Katherine said.

"Whatever," Colleen stated. "I'd take the money and run *faster*."

The waiter returned with the beer, opened the bottle and poured it into a glass. He left, then returned with a tray of assorted cheeses, Boursin, grapes and two kinds of crackers.

Colleen drummed her fingers impatiently until the waiter left. "What's the catch?" she asked.

Katherine sighed. "I must give up my life here in New York, my career, my apartment, and move to Indiana. My friends will forget me."

"You sound so melodramatic. What's the deal?" her friend demanded. "Why, just the other day you said you hated crime in the city. You got mugged for ten bucks," Colleen lectured. "You broke up with Gary. There isn't a man in your life," she continued. "Moving on to your career," Colleen said, ticking the points on her fingers, "You said yourself that your job's too stressful, and you work ridiculous hours. Plus, you're *always* complaining that your apartment is too small for you and the cats."

Katherine shrugged. "Yes, I was mugged last month for seven dollars and change. Gary is history. My job

16

sucks. My apartment is too small. But, to leave New York—my home—and my friends?"

"You're simply moving to another state," Colleen reasoned. "Trust me, your friends don't need instructions about how to get on a plane. Besides, we can talk on the phone. Or text or send emails. It's not the end of the world."

"That would be grand."

"*Grrrand*," Colleen enunciated. "You must roll your 'Rs'. Didn't you say you wanted to start your own software training business? Wouldn't Indiana be the perfect place? Don't they have a big city there?"

"The largest city is Indianapolis, but I won't be living there. My great aunt lived in a small town about a hundred miles from Indianapolis. I Googled it. It's kind of to the northwest, and sort of close to the Illinois border. There's only four thousand people in my great aunt's town."

"Four thousand people," Colleen said with disbelief. "I wonder if any of them have computers. Do you think they even have electricity?"

"Ha, ha," Katherine said, not amused.

"Just kidding," Colleen smirked. "So, cheer up. I'd be excited to get out of NYC and inherit big bucks. What's the name of this little town?"

"Erie."

Colleen drew a long breath, then belted out a loud laugh. "Eerie. Like creepy? You've got to be kidding."

"What's so funny? That's the name of it—Erie. It's named after the Erie Canal." Katherine took another sip of her Cabernet and said, "There's another provision of the will. I must take care of my great aunt's cat."

"Another cat? You've got three terrors now. Besides, wouldn't they kill each other?"

"Possibly, but probably not," Katherine kidded. "Do you remember when I brought Iris home from Magnificent Meows?"

"How can I forget. You spent all that money for a cat. In this economy? Who does that?"

"Iris was so tiny, she fit on the palm of my hand. The day I picked her up, it was snowing like crazy, so I—"

"Yes, yes. You put her inside your coat and took her home to meet Scooter, your other mink-point."

"It's Scout, not Scooter, and they're seal-point Siamese."

"Whatever," Colleen said, jokily. "How is Iris, the three-million-dollar cat? Has she scratched anyone lately?"

"No, not since Gary," Katherine laughed.

"Yeah, Gary the womanizer. Whatever possessed him to give you a third cat?"

"Why do men who cheat on their wives bring home a dozen red roses? He knew I didn't like roses, so he brought me what I cherish the most—a cat. Lilac is one of the best presents I've ever received." Katherine became very serious and returned to the main subject. "Colleen, I don't know what to do. Moving to Indiana would totally change my life, I'm sure it would. Do I really want to move out there, where I don't know anyone?"

"You know this attorney," Colleen said coyly. "How old do you think he is?"

"Why do you ask?"

"Is he young or old?"

"I don't have a clue."

"Is he married?"

"How would I know? I barely talked to the man."

"I'm sure when you move to Erie," Colleen snickered, "Mr. Lawyer will show you around and introduce you to new people."

"Very funny," Katherine commented.

"So, I think you should fly out there for a few days—meet with the attorney, see the house, visit the cat, and *then* decide whether you want to accept the big bucks."

"That's not a bad idea," Katherine agreed. "But if I go this weekend, where am I going to find a cat sitter on such short notice?"

"I'll mind the creatures," Colleen volunteered. "Of course, I don't have a clue on what to do, but you could show me. Surely it couldn't be too difficult."

Katherine laughed. "But you don't like cats."

"Oh, it's not as bad as that," Colleen protested. "Seriously, I will mind them while you're away."

"That would be great."

"This will work out perfectly for me because I have an office thing to go to Saturday night, and I'd much rather walk from your apartment in the city than take the subway from Queens."

"It's a deal. I'll buy a ticket online tonight, as soon as I get home."

"Now that I've solved your problem, why do you still have a long face?"

"How would I possibly take care of a seventeen-room house?"

"Seventeen-room house?" Colleen blurted. "Simple. You plug in the Hoover and vacuum for the rest of your life," she chuckled.

"Too funny. Let's grab a cab to my apartment and order Chinese take-out," Katherine said, cheering up.

Colleen replied, "Only if Iris is in a good mood."

"We'll pick up a can of real tuna at the bodega on the way to my apartment. She loves tuna."

The two settled their tab, then walked outside and hailed a cab. They asked the driver to stop two blocks from Katherine's apartment building. While Katherine paid the fare, Colleen darted in the bodega and bought the fish. When she came back out on the street, she said, "Tuna in oil, right?"

"Oh, no. Spring water. Oil will make them sick."

"Oops. Back in a minute," Colleen said, running back into the store.

When she returned, they both laughed, and then traded funny stories on the way to the apartment.

At the main entrance to the building, the Italian doorman ceremoniously opened the door and said, "Good evening, Ms. Kendall. I see you are in the company of your lovely friend."

"Yes, Mario," Katherine said, winking. Mario had a mild crush on Colleen.

"For the love of Mary," Colleen said, hurrying in.

"I think she likes you," Katherine whispered to Mario.

The doorman winked and began to sing a line from *Gangnam Style*. "Eh, sexy lady."

"Op, op, op, op," Katherine sang, as she did an imitation of the horsey dance.

"Oh, no way," Colleen said. "You didn't?"

"Sing it, Mario," Katherine called from the apartment mailboxes.

Colleen looked at the doorman like he had lost his mind. Mario smiled, then took a deep bow.

"This guy is a real comedian," Colleen said.

"And cute," Katherine added, putting in the good word for Mario. Katherine sorted through her mail and joked, "Publishers Clearing House—one million dollars. Drawing in February. As if I need to come into any more money."

They rode up to the top floor, giggling like school girls. As soon as they stepped off the elevator, they heard a loud wail.

"I didn't know there were any babies on your floor," Colleen commented.

"That's Scout."

"Waugh," the cat cried louder.

"I can't ever tell them apart, let alone distinguish their meows."

The activity behind the door grew noisier. One of the cats was scratching the door. Another one crashed into it.

"Hurry up with the key. They're in a frenzy, they are," Colleen said, concerned.

"Oh, for Heaven's sake. They do this every night. This is their welcoming." Katherine turned the key in the lock and then hurriedly opened the door a crack. "Hi, kids," she said to the excited cats. "Mama's home."

"Mama is home," Colleen imitated. "Auntie Colleen is here, too."

"Back. Back! Get back from the door," Katherine said to the cats as she rushed in.

Colleen came in quickly behind her. "Wow, let's feed them right away before they look at us like we're dinner."

"The can opener is in the kitchen," Katherine said.

"What? You want me to feed them?"

"Yes, it'll be good practice for this weekend."

"Well, in that case," Colleen said, heading for the kitchen. "Do they get the entire can?"

"Divide it into thirds. I'll be there in a second. Mr. Lawyer sent me the provisions of the will and I didn't get a chance to print them at the office. Katherine walked to her bedroom/office and inserted a thumb drive into the USB port. In a few seconds, she sent the files to the printer. When they finished printing, she grabbed the sheets and joined Colleen in the kitchen.

Colleen, who never spent time alone with the cats, was staring blankly at three hungry felines. Scout and Iris were on the counter, and Lilac was on the floor.

"Scout and Iris are going to love you because I never feed them on the counter," Katherine laughed. "I printed the files the attorney sent me. She handed one of the pages to Colleen and kept the other, scanning its contents.

"I give and bequeath my cat, Abigail, and the sum of one hundred thousand dollars to my great niece . . ." Colleen read out loud. "On the condition my great niece resides in my house and cares for my cat for a period of not less than twelve months."

Katherine interrupted, "It doesn't mention anything new from what he told me this morning, except if Abigail dies or is seriously harmed during the initial waiting period . . ." She stopped reading and then said, "What a terrible choice of words."

"Sounds like if anything happens to the cat, you get nothing."

"Well, that's rather doom-and-gloom."

"Plus, I see there's nothing on this page about the forty-four million dollars," Colleen said. "Are you sure you printed everything?"

"I'll check later. My head is spinning."

"Why don't you text him and ask him to send the 'tweeted' version so we can find out tonight?" Colleen laughed. "Inquiring minds need to know."

"He didn't give me his number. I'll just return his email."

"Use one of the business apps on your phone. I mean how many lawyers practice in Erie, Indiana?"

"Okay, fine," she said, fishing out her cell phone. After a few clicks, she held the phone to her ear. Scout jumped up and tried to knock the phone out of her hand.

"Hey, stop that," she said, wrestling the cat for the phone. She got the attorney's voice mail and left a message. Scout continued to butt the phone.

"Quit it," Katherine scolded. She grabbed the Siamese around the middle and put her on the floor. Scout shrieked as if she'd been injured. This set off a string of other feline events. As Scout left the room, Iris pounced on her. Scout rolled to her feet and boxed Iris's ears. Iris hissed defensively. Then the two of them ran helter-skelter into the living room. Lilac chased after them—with her tail bushed out to three times its normal size.

Colleen burst out laughing.

"Time to order Chinese," Katherine said.

The Siamese ran back into the kitchen—yowling loudly. "Chinese, not Siamese," Katherine said to the cats, punching in the take-out number.

"Cats!" Colleen exclaimed. "And to think you'll be getting another one."

Chapter Two

Katherine's plane to Indianapolis was late in taking off, which caused her to worry that Mark Dunn wouldn't wait at the airport. The attorney had promised to pick her up and drive her to Erie. She'd sent him a text message earlier, but he hadn't responded.

Once the plane landed, she texted him again, but this time he answered right back. "Head to the baggage claim area," it said. As she rode down the escalator, she struggled to pull a strand of her long black hair from the clutches of her carry-on bag. She quickly looked around the empty terminal and wished that LaGuardia had been so peaceful. She spied an elderly man with a goatee standing by the luggage carousel and assumed he was the Indiana attorney. "You must be Mr. Dunn?" she said, extending her hand.

The man grinned mischievously and said, "No, but I can pretend."

A tall, blond man in his thirties rushed over from a newspaper stand and said, "You must be Katherine. Welcome to Indiana. Did you check in any bags?"

"No, just these," she said, holding up two bags. "I'm so sorry my flight was delayed. I hope you didn't mind waiting."

"No problem. I caught up on some reading." He held up a law journal.

"Thank you so much for picking me up at the airport. I could have easily rented a car."

"No problem," he said.

"How long does it take to drive to Erie?"

"From here about an hour and a half," he said. "My car is in the parking garage. Hope you don't mind the walk."

"No, that's fine. I need to stretch my legs."

Mark took Katherine by the arm and escorted her out the baggage claim doors. "If it's any conciliation, I found a close spot. Here, let me take your bags," he offered.

"Sure, take my carry-on."

They walked a little farther, then took an elevator to the lower level. When the doors opened, he said, "Here's my car." He pointed to a green Honda Accord. "Jane Honda," he chuckled.

Katherine eyed him curiously, then laughed. "Do people out here name their cars?"

"Not sure about that, but I do," he smiled. He opened the door and put her carry-on bag on the back seat. He then motioned for Katherine to climb inside.

"It's freezing," she said, getting in.

"It's twenty-five degrees," Mark said, shutting the door. He briskly walked to the other side of the car and got in. "I made reservations at the Erie Hotel restaurant," he said, buckling up. He fired up the engine and drove out of the parking garage, then made his way to the parking attendant kiosk, where he paid. "I hope you're not vegetarian, because the Erie Hotel has been rated number one in Indiana for prime rib."

"I'm a meat and potatoes person," Katherine said, perking up at the mention of food. "Prime rib is my favorite."

"Excuse me, but I'm going to pull into the cell phone lot so I can make a few calls," he said, placing the Bluetooth hook over his right ear. Once he parked, he grabbed his Blackberry and punched in some numbers.

"That's fine," she said, gazing out the window. A jet descended noisily and appeared to be flying directly above the car. With the help of airport street lamps, she could see several inches of snow on the ground, and huge mounds of snow piled up in the parking lot. She couldn't recall ever seeing so much snow in New York.

"Erie Hotel? Yes, Velma, this is Mark Dunn. I need to change the reservation to 10:30 p.m. Thank you." He pressed the end button and dialed again. "Carol, it's Mark. I'm still in Indy. Ms. Kendall's flight was delayed. Will someone be at the front desk around midnight or a little later?" He listened, then said, "Okay. That works. We'll be at the Erie Hotel for dinner, and should be at your place before the witching hour. That's right. Okay. Bye now."

He removed the Bluetooth and then put his phone away. "No more calls," Mark promised. He put the Honda in gear and pulled out onto a service road.

"If you don't mind my asking, while you're in Indiana, who's taking care of your cats?" he asked.

"My friend Colleen's staying in my apartment for the weekend."

"Have you always lived in New York?"

"I grew up in the Bay Ridge section of Brooklyn in a townhouse built in 1890. I lived there until my mother passed away in 2009. When I took the position at Computer Net, I decided it was easier to live in the city, so I rented my current apartment."

"Doesn't it cost a lot to rent in Manhattan?"

She laughed, "Yes, quite a chunk of change. Have you always lived in Indiana?"

"Yes, born and reared. My parents own a farm near Erie. I went to Erie High School, and after I graduated, I went to Purdue, and then to the IU law school. How about you? Did you go to school?"

Twenty questions, she thought. "I went to NYU."

"What was your major? Computer Sciences, right?"

"Cadabra was with Monica for about a year when she called me, in the middle of the night, and begged me to take her. I could hear Cadabra shrieking in the background. She sounded like a wild animal. I said I wasn't sure. I'd have to think about it."

"I'm surprised," he said. "I'd think that you would jump at the opportunity to have a Siamese, considering the fact you have several now."

"I explained to Monica that I had just moved into my apartment and I was afraid Cadabra's shrieks would disturb my new neighbors."

"So how did Monica persuade you to take the Siamese?"

"The next morning, the doorman to my apartment building buzzed my intercom and said I'd better get downstairs ASAP."

As Katherine quickly sketched her first meeting with Scout for the inquisitive attorney, she gazed out the car window at the snow-covered fields, at the vague shapes of huddled trees in the distance, illuminated only by the cold winter moon and mercury vapor lamps hanging from barns and out buildings. With her voice telling the tale on autopilot, Katherine's mind replayed all the details of that day in October 2009.

"B-z-z-z-z." The intercom blared from the end of the hall. Katherine rushed to answer. She punched the button, "Yes?"

The doorman's voice answered, "Ms. Kendall, it's Mario. You'd better come downstairs right away. This lady dropped off a present for you, and it's screaming."

She pressed the talk button, "A screaming present? That's a first. Coming right down."

Katherine waited impatiently for the elevator, and when it hadn't come in what seemed like an eternity, she rushed to the stairwell and bolted down twenty-two flights of stairs. She flew out the service door leading to the marble-floored lobby, luxuriously decorated with colonial furnishings. Mario, the Italian doorman with jet-black hair and blue eyes, wore a concerned expression on his face.

"What is it?" Katherine asked, out of breath.

"I think it's a cat," he said.

Mario had placed the cat carrier right on top of his reception desk at the front entrance.

Katherine peered inside. "It's a Siamese. Did a woman named Monica DeSutter bring this?" she demanded, hand-on-hip.

"Hiss," the cat inside the carrier snarled.

"I'm sorry. I didn't get her name," Mario apologized. "She did say the cat's name was Cada . . ."

"Cadabra," Katherine finished.

The Siamese began rocking the cat carrier back and forth and wailing in shrill, mournful cries.

"I don't think it likes that name," Mario suggested.

"She," Katherine corrected. "Cadabra is a girl cat."

The Siamese emitted a throaty growl.

The elevator doors opened and the wealthy Mrs. Pendleton got off and bustled toward the front door. She made a dead stop in front of Mario's desk.

"Ah, Mrs. Pendleton, good morning. Your limo is waiting," he said dutifully.

"What is that creature, and what has possessed it to make that dreadful noise?" she sniffed haughtily.

"I beg your pardon, but that creature is a Siamese," Katherine said icily.

Cadabra rolled onto her back and began kicking the top of the cat carrier. She crossed her eyes and began to salivate like a rabid animal.

"I thought the board had a policy about permitting wild animals in the building," Mrs. Pendleton huffed.

Cadabra snarled fiercely.

"Well, I never," Mrs. Pendleton said indignantly. Mario held the door open for her and she stormed out of the building.

Cadabra immediately turned over and nuzzled the metal gate on the front of the cat carrier. She began purring.

Mario and Katherine burst out laughing. "This cat is a born actress," Mario observed.

"That was the best cat fit I've ever seen," Katherine added.

"Ms. Kendall," Mark said, interrupting the reverie.

"Oh, I'm sorry," Katherine said, waking from her reverie. "What were you saying?"

"When did you decide to name her 'Scout?'"

"A few days after I got her. At night she patrols my apartment like she's on a reconnaissance mission. She's prowled so much, she's developed calluses on her paws."

"What other tricks does Scout do, besides answering phones?"

"When you say Abracadabra, she arches her back and dances like a Halloween cat."

"You're kidding," Mark said.

"I don't say it very often because it seems to upset her."

"Maybe it brings back a sad memory."

"I also have a seal-point named Iris, and she's my resident cat burglar. She steals my cosmetic brushes and stashes them under my bed. Lilac, my two-year-old lilac-point, fetches a three-inch, stuffed toy bear."

"Cats don't fetch," he said skeptically.

"Lilac does. She fetches until she drops in exhaustion. I have to put the bear away."

"You really like your cats," he said. "I really like mine, too."

"You have a cat?" she asked, surprised.

"I have a Maine Coon," he answered proudly. "He's about four-years-old."

"Iris is four."

Mark said slyly, "He's been fixed."

"Iris has been spayed, but she loves to flirt."

"Is there any way we can convince you to stay longer than a weekend?" Mark asked, changing the subject.

"I'll be here two full days. My plane leaves at 6:00 p.m. on Sunday."

"That doesn't give us very much time."

"I think it's enough time. I'm prepared to give you my answer in forty-eight hours or less," she said. "What's on the agenda for me? Where will I be staying? When do I get to meet Abigail?"

"Dinner with me tonight. You'll be staying in Erie's only bed and breakfast, the Little Tomato."

"Little Tomato?" Katherine asked curiously. "What kind of a name is that?"

"Indiana is known for its tomatoes. Have you ever had one?"

"No, I'm afraid not, but I could have eaten one and not known it," she snickered.

"It's possible," he chuckled. "Back to the bed and breakfast, the building is over a hundred-years-old and is listed on the National Register."

"Does it have electricity?"

"Yes. And heat and hot water," he quipped, "The owner of the Little Tomato is a friend of mine. She also owns one of the antique stores downtown. If you think the name of her B&B is funny, wait until I tell you *her* name."

"What's her name?"

"Carol Lombard."

"Like the movie actress?"

"Yes. Doesn't every town have one?"

"Does the B & B have Wi-Fi? I brought my laptop so I can check my email."

"I think so, but don't know how strong the signal will be. It varies."

"I guess I'll find out," she answered. "When do I meet Abigail?"

"Tomorrow morning around nine. I'll pick you up at a quarter 'til, and we'll drive out to the vet's office so you can meet the little charmer. The vet's name is Sonny Hunter, but everyone calls him Dr. Sonny."

"Why doesn't he go by 'Dr. Hunter'?"

"Because his father is also a vet, and he goes by 'Dr. Hunter'," he answered. "After you meet Abigail, I'll give you a tour of your great aunt's house and introduce you to the two employees who are taking care of her—"

"Her? My great aunt's house is a 'she'?"

"Orvenia called her house 'Vicky'."

"Ah, for Victorian. What are the names of the two employees?"

"Vivian Marston and Cokey Cokenberger. Vivian is the housekeeper, and Cokey is the handyman. Mr. Cokenberger also has his own general contracting business. He's employed by the estate to maintain the house. He's undertaking a major project right now, repairing masonry in the basement."

"I'm very anxious to meet Abigail and to see the house, but afterward can we visit my great aunt's crypt?"

"Yes, by all means. The mausoleum is about thirty miles from Erie."

"Thanks," she smiled. "I'm not sure if you're aware, but my great aunt was my mother's only aunt on the maternal side," Katherine offered. "My mother passed away from cancer in 2009, and my father died a year later."

"I'm sorry to hear that you've lost both your parents."

She hesitated for a moment, then said, "You mentioned that your parents own a farm."

"Oh, yes, but my dad wants to retire soon. Mom is a teacher at the elementary school. She's eager to retire, also. I have a sister in California, and a brother who lives in Minnesota. My grandmother lives in a retirement community close to Erie; she's ninety-years-old."

"That's nice," she smiled.

They continued talking throughout the trip. Katherine thought he was very easy to talk to, and fun to be with. She was having such a good time, she hadn't even noticed that an hour and a half had passed until she saw the sign: Erie Town Limits.

"This is Erie," Mark said, slowing down.

"I wish it were light outside," she complained. "I'll have to wait until tomorrow to really get a good look at things."

Mark began pointing out key businesses. "Over there is the funeral home. There's the ice cream stand."

"Granny Sleeps Here," Katherine chuckled, reading the marquee. "I hope the ice cream is better than the name. It looks boarded-up to me. Granny must be asleep?"

"It's seasonal. There's the video store. There's one of the local restaurants. We're getting very close to Orvenia's house."

"Is it on this street? Which side?" she asked anxiously.

"It's several blocks down on Lincoln Street."

"Can you drive by the house before we go to dinner? I'm dying to see it."

"Better yet," he said. "Behind the grain elevator there's a service alley that leads to Lincoln Street. This alley provides the best vantage point for viewing the front of the house. However, it's so dark outside, I'm not quite sure you'll be able to truly see the house," he said. He turned the car, drove a short distance, then stopped in front of a large Victorian house. "There she is," he announced. "Vicky is the most exquisite house in Erie."

Katherine was momentarily speechless. The house seemed larger than she'd imagined. "This is the house," she finally said. "I've never seen a house so big. I am to live here? I'd get lost."

Mark pulled out onto the street. "You'll get to see the inside tomorrow," he said, pulling back onto the main highway. "Most of the houses on this street are in the historic district. It's one of the few remaining tree-lined streets. Most of the trees are maples, and at least a hundred years old. During the fall, many locals and out-of-towners walk down Lincoln Street, snapping photos of the autumn leaves. There's a walking guide that's printed by the State Division of Tourism. Oh, yes, there's a park nearby, with walking and hiking trails. Near the parking lot, there's a gazebo that was built in the 1890s. In the summer, visiting bands come and perform on Saturday evenings."

"I'm fascinated," she said. "What about crime here?"

Mark laughed. "Our last murder was eleven years ago, and theft or burglary are virtually non-existent. Driving while intoxicated is a problem, which doesn't surprise me because there are more bars in Erie than there are churches."

"I never thought of comparing the two," she said.

"Suffice it to say, there are seven taverns for four thousand people," he said almost apologetically. "Here we are." He parked outside the restaurant and got out of the car.

Katherine waited for him to open her door.

"Welcome to downtown Erie," he said, helping her out of the car. "The restaurant is in a hotel that was built in 1888."

She gazed up at its blue and lavender-painted corbels.

"Let's go inside. It's freezing out here," he said, slapping his gloved hands together.

"No, just a second." Katherine adjusted the collar on her wool coat and slowly peered down the street. The town seemed to be a mecca of antique shops, in well-maintained Victorian-era storefronts, constricted to a two-block area. She was enchanted. Finally, she said, "This town looks like a miniature model railroad town."

"Except our trees have leaves and not lichens," he joked. "Seriously, the town is unique because so many townspeople are restoring old homes."

Mark opened the heavy wooden door of the hotel.

Katherine walked inside and observed the antique shop on the left and the restaurant on the right. Several people were browsing in the antique shop.

"This way," he directed. He led her to a foyer outside the main serving room. The room was dimly lit by the glow of a gas log burning in the fireplace. Every available wall space was covered with old family portraits framed in vintage gold frames.

"Allow me to take your coat," he said. "I must warn you. If you order the prime rib, you must wear a bib."

"A bib—like a baby's bib?" she asked.

"Yes, but much bigger. It's a tradition here."

"Okay. Why not," she said. "But you wouldn't catch me dead with one of those things in Manhattan."

The hostess entered the room and smiled. "Hello, Mark. Is this Orvenia's niece?"

"Yes," Katherine smiled. "I'm Katherine Kendall."

"Welcome to Erie Hotel," the hostess smiled and extended her hand. "My name is Velma Richardson."

Katherine shook her hand.

"I'm so sorry to hear about dear Mrs. Colfax. It was a great shock to all of us. We thought that she'd live forever."

The woman escorted them to their candlelit table.

"Were you a friend of my great aunt's?" Katherine inquired.

"No, just an acquaintance. We were part of the same church congregation," she said. Velma turned to Mark. "I'm helping Patricia out with the drinks tonight— she's your server this evening, but is busy with that large table over there," she motioned. "What would you like to drink?"

"I'll have a seltzer, please," Katherine said.

"I think I might have an antacid in my pocket-book," the hostess answered.

"Seltzer," Katherine grinned. "Sparkling water. Do you have any?"

"We have town water," the hostess said slowly. "And nearby there's a spring where they still cap the water."

"It's called Mudlavia Springs," Mark said. "It's a national company."

"Yes, I've heard of it. Okay, I'll have a glass of that, and also a glass of Cabernet."

"Caber-what?" the hostess seemed perplexed.

"Wine," Katherine answered.

"We have white wine, merlot—"

Katherine interrupted, "Merlot is fine."

"And you, Mr. Dunn?" the hostess asked.

"I'll have some of that wonderful town water with a slice of lemon."

The hostess winked at Mark and left. He tipped his head back and laughed. His green eyes sparkled.

"What's so funny?"

"I'm sure there's a lot of things this town can learn from you. Your presence would be an asset to the town."

"Flattery will get you nowhere," she scoffed.

The drinks arrived and the couple toasted the future.

Mark said, "May you move to our fine town and live happily ever after."

Katherine countered, "May I move to this fine town and my cats have nine lives."

Their glasses clinked.

The server came over to the table, said hello to Mark, then introduced herself to Katherine. "My name is Patricia Marston. I'm the daughter of your great aunt's housekeeper—Vivian's daughter."

"I'm pleased to meet you."

"For the last five years I've taken care of Orvenia's garden during my school summer breaks," she said in a monotone voice.

"Where do you go to school?"

"The university in the city," she said. "I'm a graduate student."

"What do you major in?" Katherine asked.

"Botany," Patricia answered. "Now, what can I get you this evening?"

"We would both like the prime rib," Mark said.

The server smiled slightly, wrote down their order, and returned to the kitchen.

Katherine took a sip of her wine. "I have a question for you. Where was the housekeeper when my great aunt died?"

Mark looked surprised, then relaxed. "Orvenia died in the middle of the night. Mrs. Marston found her the following morning."

"Did she cry out, or ask for assistance in any way?"

"She might have, but nobody was in the house to hear her, or to call an ambulance."

"I thought Mrs. Marston and her daughter lived in the house," Katherine said.

"No," Mark answered. "Vivian has an apartment downtown. After Orvenia passed away, Vivian moved into the house, but this arrangement is only temporary. Patricia rents a room at the Erie Hotel. Orvenia lived quite alone for most of her life. She preferred it that way."

"My mother didn't talk much about her aunt. You must understand my great aunt moved to Indiana before my mom was even born. I think they exchanged Christmas cards every year, but that was the extent of their relationship. I suppose that since you're my great aunt's attorney, you're probably aware of the big scandal?"

"Scandal?" he asked.

"Mom said she was a beautiful woman with lots of suitors, but she chose to run off with an older man in his late 70s. Didn't he die soon thereafter?"

"I believe it was about a year later. William was eighty when he died," Mark offered.

Katherine observed Mark's bland expression and said, "That was the scandal. My great aunt was seventeen when she married him."

"Well, you know," he said, looking down at the table, "a lot of people in this town thought Orvenia was a gold-digger. When William married her, he immediately changed his will. If he died first, Orvenia would inherit everything. Previously, he had been inclined to leave his wealth to the town."

"I feel sorry for my great aunt. Poor thing, disowned by her family back in Brooklyn, and then not accepted by the townspeople. Did she ever talk about my great uncle to you?"

"Yes, she did. In fact, she must have cared deeply for him, because she never remarried. Tomorrow I'll make sure to show you his portrait."

Patricia brought the steaks over. "Sorry it took so long," she said, putting the hot plates down. "Don't touch that steak until I come back," she commanded. She rushed to the kitchen, and then returned with two bibs. Katherine protested slightly, but then acquiesced to the town tradition.

Chapter Three

Half-asleep, Katherine sat up in bed and strained to look around the room, which was enveloped in darkness. *It's too dark*, she thought. She listened for the ordinary street noises. There were no blaring police car sirens echoing down Lexington Avenue to the east. There were no wailing car alarms triggered by a driver parallel parking, or a thunderclap. Where was the sanitation truck, with its noisy clanging and banging, screeching and thumping? It seemed to be way past his usual pick-up time of three o'clock in the morning. Even the pigeons were not cooing outside on her twenty-second-floor window ledge.

Katherine began to panic. Where are the cats? "Lilac . . . Scout . . . Iris," she called. She felt for them in the dark, and then realized they weren't there, because she wasn't even in New York state, let alone cuddled up with the Siamese in her warm bed. Instead, she was lying in a four-poster canopy bed in a bed and breakfast called the Little Tomato, in faraway Indiana.

She stumbled out of bed and searched for the light switch. She walked into a chair. "Ouch," she moaned, as she struggled to find the wall. She cursed aloud, then stepped on her carry-on bag. Finally, she found the switch for the ceiling light fixture. The dim light from the low wattage bulb cast eerie shadows on the wall. She picked up her watch. I read five a.m.

The room was incredibly cold. Katherine lamented that she hadn't brought her fuzzy bathrobe or her slippers, but congratulated herself for packing her heavy-duty fleece pajamas, which, she surmised, had prevented her from freezing to death. She jumped back into bed and pulled the covers over her, shivering.

She thought about the cats. During the workweek, 5:00 in the morning was their usual wake-up time. Katherine would get up and feed the cats, then would get ready for work. By the time she'd finished putting on her make-up, fixed her hair, and put on her clothes, the cats would be stretched out languidly next to the steam heat radiator.

That's it, she thought. *I'm freezing in my bed and I'm subconsciously trying to get warm by thinking about my apartment's steam heat.* She vowed to never complain again about the temperature in the living room being 82 degrees in the middle of winter. She wondered if she could ever get used to the Indiana cold.

She forced herself out of bed and ventured into the hallway. She found the communal bathroom and went inside, bolting the door lock behind her. She took a hot shower and then returned to her room to get dressed. While she was out of the room, someone—the note said, "compliments of the house"—had placed a warm coffeepot on the nightstand with a large, heavily iced sweet roll.

She took one bite and said out loud, "This is incredible."

She put the roll down and wiped her sticky fingers on a paper napkin. She fished her cell phone out of her bag and started to call Colleen to check on her cats, but then she realized how early it was and decided Colleen would be fast asleep. *Stop worrying*, she thought. Colleen may be totally new at cat care, but she was smart enough to figure it out. Siamese had clever ways of dealing with newcomers, and showing them the ropes.

Mark arrived at nine o'clock. Because he was fifteen minutes late, Katherine had put on her coat and was waiting for him at the front door. When she saw him pull up, she hurried outside. He jumped out of his car and opened the door for her.

"I'm sorry I'm late," he apologized.

"No problem," she said.

"One of my clients called right as I was about to leave, and I had to answer a few quick questions that ended up taking more time." He went on to explain that the veterinarian office was located a mile north of Erie. "How did you like your room?" he asked cheerfully.

"It was great. I think I was the only guest staying at the Tomato last night."

"Business is probably pretty slow this time of year," he agreed.

"This morning, while I was taking a shower, someone brought coffee to my room and the most fantastic cinnamon roll ever," she said, engaging in simple chitchat. "It was delicious."

"That must have been Carol. Her cinnamon rolls are known throughout the county. That was thoughtful of her."

"It was huge and sticky and covered with a mountain of icing," Katherine continued.

"You're making me hungry. I haven't had breakfast," Mark said.

"Sorry. May I treat you to lunch today?" she offered.

"I'd be delighted," he replied.

"I cannot wait to meet Abigail," Katherine said excitedly.

"She's a sweet cat," Mark said.

"If she's so sweet, then why doesn't she stay with you?" Katherine asked.

"My Maine Coon weighs twenty-five pounds and is very bossy. I was afraid he might hurt her."

"Does he routinely beat up other cats?"

"I really don't know. He's never come into contact with another cat. However, he's very jealous of my women friends, and a female cat might really upset him."

"What's your cat's name?" she asked, as Mark pulled into a long gravel road leading to the vet's office.

"I named him Bruiser after a famous Hoosier wrestler named Dick the Bruiser. When Bruiser was a few months old—my cat, that is—he managed to push my forty-six-inch flat-screen off the entertainment center, so I've called him Bruiser ever since."

Mark pulled in front of the veterinary clinic and parked the car. A sign over the door read: "Please wipe your paws."

Katherine hurriedly opened the car door and darted inside the clinic. She announced her name to the receptionist, who quickly showed her to an empty examination room. Mark followed the two women inside.

"Dr. Sonny will be with you in a moment," the receptionist said. "Please have a seat and make yourselves comfortable." She closed the door behind her.

After a few minutes, Katherine began to fidget. "I hate to wait."

"A New Yorker hating to wait," he grinned.

"Yes, we hate a line just as much as anyone."

The door opened and a white-smocked man walked inside, carrying a small, rusty-brown bundle of fur. "Hello," he said. The cat nestled deeper into the crook of his arm. "I'm Dr. Sonny," he said to Katherine. "And my little friend here is Abigail. She's very shy at first, but once she warms up to you, she's quite affectionate."

Katherine stood up. "She's beautiful. I love her gold eyes. Can I hold her?"

"By all means," he said, unhooking Abigail's claws from his jacket. He finally dislodged the clinging cat and placed the Abyssinian in the arms of her prospective caretaker.

"She seems terrified," Katherine said. "She's trembling."

"I'm sure she'll be fine after a while," Mark said.

"I'll let the two of you get acquainted. I have an emergency surgery coming in a few minutes," Dr. Sonny said. "When you're finished visiting, just let Valerie at reception know, and she'll return Abigail to her cage." He smiled, then left the room.

"She's so tiny," Katherine said.

"Petite," Mark noted.

Katherine cradled Abigail in her arms and began to gently knead the fur on the back of the Abyssinian's neck. Abigail began purring loudly and slowly blinked her eyes. "Do you know what that means?" Katherine asked.

"That you're choking her," Mark observed.

"No," she laughed. "When a cat squeezes its eyes it's actually blowing you a kiss." She kissed the purring bundle on her head. "How old did you say she is?"

"About two."

"She can't weigh but six pounds. She's as light as a feather."

"Never judge a cat by its weight. I've seen this cat in action. Orvenia thought Abby was part-monkey, always climbing to the top of furniture. Her favorite place is on top of a tall window valance."

"This little creature?" Katherine said. "I can't imagine her doing anything but sleeping." The cat looked up and chirped.

"Did you hear that?" Katherine said. "She sounds like a bird."

"Abyssinians are generally very quiet cats—at least that's what the breeder said in Wisconsin. They're notorious for being hyperactive. She might be lethargic now because she has been boarded in a cage with limited exercise."

Katherine sat down and continued cradling the Abyssinian.

"I think Abigail is going to sleep," he said.

"Did you know that Abyssinians are supposedly descendants of the Egyptian sacred cat?" The little cat opened her eyes and looked soulfully up at Katherine, then began to purr loudly again. "I looked it up on the Internet."

"This is a good sign—two bouts of purring," Mark said. "I think she likes you."

"You're quite the salesman," Katherine kidded. "I think I like her, too," she said stroking the cat's silky fur.

"Do I take it you've decided to accept your great aunt's offer?"

Katherine kissed the resting cat on the head. "I'm seriously considering it, but permit me to make up my mind after I've seen the house."

"It's a deal. I'll get Valerie to take Abigail, and we can go straight to the house," Mark said, opening the door. He called the receptionist.

Valerie came in and took the cat from Katherine. The Abyssinian looked up, squeezed her eyes, then chirped.

"Say good-bye, Abby," Valerie said as she picked up the cat and walked out of the room.

"I'm in love," Katherine said. "She's truly wonderful."

"I hope you feel the same way about the house," Mark said, escorting Katherine to the car. "Would you prefer to have a cup of coffee first?" he said, deliberately trying to hide his enthusiasm. "It ain't Starbucks," he mocked "but there's a diner a few miles from here."

"What did you say?" she said dreamily.

"Coffee. Caffeine. Latte! Cappuccino!"

She didn't answer until they were back on the highway. "Yes, coffee would be fine, but after I see the house."

They drove on in silence. Once on Lincoln Street, Katherine began to admire the historic houses. "These houses are gigantic."

"The brick house on the corner is an Italianate built in the 1870s," Mark said, pointing. "Over there is a Classical Revival."

"I can imagine their utility bills."

"And this is Orvenia's former home. The locals still refer to it as the William Colfax house." He pulled into the drive and parked under a covered carport known as a porte cochère.

She was silent for a moment, then said, "I didn't realize the house was pink."

"Orvenia was fascinated by the Victorian painted ladies in San Francisco, and like so many of the houses there, she wanted this one to have a four-color paint scheme."

Katherine got out of the car and began walking around the perimeter of the house. She gazed up at the three stories, taking in the many architectural features—the cross-gabled roof, the fish-scale-shingled turret, the stained glass in several windows, the front porch columns, the limestone pillars, and the maroon arches framing the covered carport. She rejoined Mark, who was now standing on the bottom step of the side entrance.

"Look here," Mark said, pointing up at the ornate brass doorbell. "You'll find that many of the original details still remain in the house."

"It's incredible."

"Ready to go inside?"

She nodded.

He offered his arm. "Shall we?" Together they walked up the stairs. On the top step he fumbled for a key, then turned it in the ancient lock. He pushed the heavy door open. "This way," he said, directing Katherine from the small foyer to a large, formal dining room.

"The ceilings are so high," she said.

"Thirteen feet," he said.

"I love the burgundy wallpaper."

"It was silk-screened."

"And a chair rail. Lilac would love this."

"Look above," Mark said. "There's also a plate rail."

"What a gorgeous plate collection. Surely my great aunt didn't get up on a ladder every time she set the table,"

Katherine chuckled. "Just kidding. I can see Lilac now, hurling the dishes off of her new cat walk."

"Do your cats break a lot of things?"

"Not really," she said. "Sometimes there are accidents, but I've learned not to cherish an object that can one moment be admired, and then later broken into smithereens."

Mark smiled and said, "I'll show you the rest of the house, but first let me check the basement to see if Mr. Cokenberger is working. He's the handyman I mentioned. He's more familiar with the house than I am." Mark disappeared into another part of the house.

Katherine walked into the next room, which was as richly decorated and lavishly furnished as the dining room. She was amazed that the ceiling was decorated as ornately as the walls. The frieze paper above the picture rail depicted blue and green peacocks. Against one wall was a crystal vase full of peacock feathers atop a marble-top curio cabinet, which was centered between two kerosene-light wall sconces made of intricately etched brass. Next to the vase was a small, flat-screen TV, which seemed to be a curious anachronism compared to the Victorian-era furnishings throughout the room.

She admired the gilded mirrors and antique lithographs that hung by brass chains and molding hooks from picture rails. A red oriental rug, octagonal in shape, lay in the center of the room. Beyond the rug's edges was a geometric-patterned, wood parquet floor. An octagonal table rested on the rug, with the day's mail scattered on the tabletop. Katherine counted five wide pocket doors, all of them closed.

To Katherine's right, a great staircase was carpeted with the same red oriental carpeting. Brass rods held the carpet in place against each riser. Katherine's eyes followed the stairs to each landing. Where the handrail met a newel post, there was a carved acorn ornament. At each of the staircase's three turns, the newel post's acorn was carved slightly smaller than the one at the previous landing.

The first landing had an oblong window with a floral-garland pattern in rose-colored stained glass. The winter-morning light filtered through the glass and scattered rose-colored shades of light on the parquet floor. A maroon crystal chandelier hung from a satin-covered chain. Its dim light cast curious waves and sunbursts of color on the gold-textured ceiling.

Mark joined her in the room. "Orvenia called this room the atrium. What do you think so far?" he said.

"It's like I just went back in time," Katherine replied.

They continued the tour of the house. Mark escorted Katherine into the gold-damask-wallpapered parlor, where flames blazed in the fireplace.

"What a grand fireplace," she commented. "But why is the mirror so high?"

"Mirrors were placed high to increase the illumination of the gas-light fixtures."

"Let's see," Katherine began to muse. "If we move the ceramic vases from the two sconces, I can see Lilac and Abigail perched on each—sitting back on their haunches like two mismatched bookends. Iris would be sitting in front of the fireplace, basking in the glow of the warm fire."

"What about the magic cat? What would she be doing?"

"She'd stroll in for a moment, groom the top of Iris's head, and then resume her house patrolling," she said. "By the way, who's minding the fire?" Katherine asked.

"Oh, that's not a wood-burning fireplace. It's a gas log. You turn it on and off with a switch," he explained.

"Good to know," she answered.

"Mrs. Marston should be down in a minute. She's temporarily living in the house; she has full reign of the upstairs," Mark said.

"The entire floor?" Katherine asked.

"No, just two of the rooms and a bathroom toward the back of the house. There are three other bedrooms besides those she occupies. A set of stairs in the back lead to the first-floor kitchen from Mrs. Marston's section."

"There's something that doesn't make any sense to me. Why doesn't Mrs. Marston take care of Abigail?"

"She's been suffering from migraine headaches. I've hired a temporary housekeeper to replace her while she's been ill."

"How long has that been?"

"Just a few weeks. Mrs. Marston has agreed to stay on here until we can find the individual who'll move into this house. I'm hoping that person will be you," Mark said, beaming. "Mrs. Marston wishes to move back into her apartment soon. You see, your great aunt set up a trust for her in the amount of two hundred thousand dollars," he said. He whispered, "I think she's anxious to have access to that money."

Katherine momentarily looked shocked, then said, "Will I meet her today?"

As if on cue, Katherine heard a creak from the floorboards of the nearby stairs. She stepped back into the atrium and saw a woman in her mid-sixties descend the stairs.

"Hello," the woman greeted. "You must Katherine."

"Yes, and you must be Mrs. Marston."

"Vivian," the woman corrected. "Mrs. Colfax called me Viv. I hope you had a pleasant flight. The weather forecast predicts twelve inches of snow tomorrow. I hope that doesn't hinder your getting about and seeing our fine town."

"Twelve inches," Katherine worried. "I hope I don't get snowed in here. I have a very important meeting on Monday."

"I wouldn't fret. The town is quite efficient about clearing the streets," Mrs. Marston replied.

"The main highways are rarely closed," Mark added.

"My daughter Patricia will be here soon. I want you to meet her."

"She was at the restaurant last night, and Katherine met her then," he said.

"She seems very bright. You must be very proud," Katherine commented.

"She's very smart in school. She's also very talented in the garden. Mrs. Colfax loved her herb garden. Sometimes my daughter would bake her signature black walnut cake. Your great aunt adored it. As a matter-of-fact, I do, too. She baked one last night. Would you care for some? When Patricia comes, I'll ask her to make us some tea," she offered.

"No, that's not necessary, Vivian," Mark said. "We're going to have coffee later."

"It was so nice meeting you, Ms. Kendall, and seeing you again, Mr. Dunn. If you'll excuse me, I must return upstairs. I haven't been feeling very well lately."

"Shall I help you upstairs?" Mark asked.

"If you don't mind. I've been getting dizzy spells, and I don't like the idea of falling down these stairs." She forced a laugh.

He rushed to her side and took her arm. They slowly ascended the stairs.

Katherine said good-bye, then slid open one of the pocket doors in the atrium. It opened to a living room crammed full of Victorian furniture. A rosewood sofa and matching loveseat were upholstered in mauve velvet. Nearby were gentleman's and lady's chairs covered in pink brocade. There were several ornately carved, walnut Rococo parlor tables; a few of the tables had marble tops. In one corner, a tall, walnut Renaissance Revival étagère had six shelves holding a collection of Lladro *Mother and Child* figurines. To the right of the fireplace was a huge portrait. Mark came into the room and stood beside her.

"Is that William?" she asked.

"Yes. William Colfax III."

"Handsome man. No wonder my great aunt married him."

"I take it you fancy dark-haired men with blue eyes," Mark said, and then laughed. "I'd say your great uncle was in his thirties when this portrait was painted."

"So, in reality, my great aunt fell in love with a man with snow-white hair and blue eyes."

"You stand corrected."

"Is Mrs. Marston going to be okay?"

"I think so."

"Has she gone to a doctor?"

"No, she is quite stubborn. I'm hoping her daughter will persuade her to at least see a physician and possibly have some tests done."

"Thanks for rescuing me from the walnut cake."

"What do you mean?"

"I'm allergic to walnuts."

At the end of the long, narrow room, a door opened and a man in his late forties walked in. He was wearing a Yankees cap. He tipped his cap and said, "I just wanted to make you feel at home."

Katherine smiled. "You must be Mr. Cokenberger?"

He extended his hand. "Cokey," he said.

Mark said, "Cokey has single-handedly done most of the restoration on this house."

"That's quite impressive," Katherine said.

"I'm sorry for your loss," Cokey said to Katherine. "I worked for Mrs. Colfax for the past seven years. She was a great lady."

"Are you going to be working much longer in the basement?" Mark asked him.

"At least another week tuck-pointing. The interior wall bricks in the turret area have to be re-pointed from the floor up."

"What's tuck-pointing?" she asked.

"It means you remove the crumbling mortar between the bricks, then put in new. It takes a lot of time," the handyman answered.

"Do you live in Erie?" Katherine said, making small talk.

Cokey nodded. "I live a few streets over on Alexander Street. I have a key to the basement-level entrance at the back of the house. I come and go. I fix things, run errands, change light bulbs. Sometimes I'd drive Mrs. Colfax into the city and wait while she shopped. We'd stop at one of her favorite restaurants and have lunch."

"One more question," she said. "Has this house been rewired? I have a lot of computer equipment, and I wouldn't want to blow any fuses."

"The electrical system is state-of-the-art, 200-amp, and up-to-code. I installed it," Cokey said proudly. "It was nice meeting you. I need to get back. I just mixed a batch of mortar downstairs, and I need to use it before it sets." The handyman left the room, leaving a trail of dusty footprints on the navy-blue oriental rug.

When he was no longer within earshot, Katherine said, "I don't like that 'have-my-own-key business, come-and-go.' I'd want to know who's in the house at all times. It would be easy for crims to hide out in this place."

"Crims?" Mark asked.

She chuckled. "Criminals. Does Mrs. Marston tidy up after this man? Look at that rug."

"You seem to be just like Orvenia," he winked. "She was a cleaning machine."

"You learn to be tidier than usual when you have as many cats as I do."

"That makes sense," he said. "Allow me to show you the rest of the house. Let's begin with the room in the back of the house. It has wood floors and oak wainscoting. It opens onto a carpeted sun porch. I think this room would provide a perfect home office space."

"Can I see the kitchen first?" she asked.

"Sure," he said, opening a door from the dining room that led into a 1950s kitchen, complete with red Formica table, matching chrome chairs, aqua metal cabinets, and a black-and-white ceramic tile floor.

"I love it," Katherine exclaimed. "Even the stove is from the '50s."

"We could always replace it," he said.

"Are you kidding? My family's stove in Brooklyn looked like this. I hope it's gas."

"Right you are," he said.

The tour continued for another thirty minutes. Mark showed Katherine every nook and cranny of the old house—the rear stairs from the kitchen, Orvenia Colfax's bedroom and sitting rooms, and the guest rooms—all crammed full of Victorian furniture and adornments. She particularly enjoyed the attic, with its trunks of memorabilia and the gargoyle that stood sentry by the east window under a small floodlight fixture.

"It's so cool that my great aunt has a gargoyle," she said, amused.

"Orvenia told me it guards the house against water damage. Plus, I think she bought it as a joke for the neighborhood kids. They look upon this house as being haunted."

"Well, is it?" she asked. "Are there any ghosts?"

"You have my solemn word that there are no ghosts in this house," he said, with a hint of forced formality.

"If there are, my friend Colleen will find them. She's an administrative assistant by day, and a paranormal investigator by night."

"A ghost hunter?" he asked, slightly amused.

"She belongs to the Irish chapter in NY."

"Interesting," he said, non-committedly.

"There are so many trunks up here," she said, changing the subject. She opened one and found stacks of papers—receipts, bills of lading—the usual accounting files. Leaning against the wall was a tall, rectangular shape, covered with an old tablecloth. Katherine went over and removed the cloth, which sent a cloud of fine dust into the air. She coughed, then exclaimed, "What a lovely portrait. Who's this woman?"

Mark came over. "Why, I've never seen this before. The woman would have to be related to you, because I can see a resemblance. She's got your dark hair and green eyes—"

"This is uncanny. This has to be my great aunt when she was younger. How can we find out?"

Mark turned the oil painting around and scrutinized the back. On the bottom of the canvas was a handwritten note. "You're right. It's your great aunt."

"What does it say?"

"Orvenia Colfax—1932."

"Wouldn't it be lovely to hang her portrait in the living room?"

"Where would you put William's?"

"It can stay where it is. We could put my great aunt's portrait on the other side of the fireplace."

"Consider it done," he said.

"Oh, what am I saying? I'm acting as if I'm moving into this house."

"I hope you do," he said seriously.

"Perhaps," she said. "Here, help me put this cloth back over it."

They walked back downstairs, and Katherine watched Mark turn off the gas supply to the parlor fireplace.

"Just in case Mrs. Marston forgets," he said, extinguishing the flame. When he finished, he announced he was going to the basement to mention something to the handyman. While Mark was away, Katherine milled about the parlor, admiring her great aunt's impressive Chinese cloisonné collection on the fireplace mantel. She was startled to hear Mrs. Marston and another woman arguing upstairs.

"Leave him alone. He's a married man," Mrs. Marston demanded.

"He was promised to me before she came into the picture," a woman's voice said.

"Lower your voice. She'll hear you. I saw that Jimson Weed growing in the plant room, and a bag of seeds sitting next to it for anyone to see."

"How did you know what it was?" replied the other woman, haughtily.

"I wasn't born yesterday. That stuff used to grow wild on the farm. It can kill you! I know that young people are ending up in ERs all over the country because of it. Are you abusing drugs again?"

"Don't be ridiculous. I'm growing that as a part of my final research paper this semester."

"Then take it to the university, but wherever you take it, I want that damned plant out of this house today, you hear me?"

"Whatever," the other voice said dismissively. "I'll take it out when *that* woman leaves."

"Where are you going? Come back here. I'm not done talking to you," Mrs. Marston said angrily.

A door slammed, and then another.

The woman must have taken the rear stairs,
Katherine thought. She hurried to the kitchen to head her
off at the foot of the stairs, but was stopped by Mark
outside the dining room door.

"Are you ready to go?" he asked.

"Oh, yes," she said, startled. She hesitated for a
moment, then said cheerily, trying to mask her curiosity, "I
just heard Mrs. Marston talking to someone upstairs."

"Patricia's here. I saw her car parked out back. Did
you want to speak to her before we leave?"

"Oh, no. That's okay," she said. "But I overheard a
conversation between the two of them, something about a
dangerous weed."

"Dangerous weed," he said, startled. "I'll look into
it."

"Listen, Mark, if I accept the terms of the will and
move out here with my cats, I don't want something like
that in the house."

"Understood. So, let's carry on. There's more to
see."

The day went on. Mark showed Katherine every
piece of real estate and landmark in the town. He even
showed her where he lived—a sprawling, ranch-style house
a few streets away from the Colfax mansion on Lincoln
Street.

She was immediately shocked by the size of his cat, and remarked that he looked more like a tiger than a Maine Coon. While Mark pulled out his Blackberry and called the B&B's owner to suggest more heat, Katherine remained on the sofa and petted his cat. The Maine Coon had taken an immediate liking to her. His loud purr rivaled the sound of a jet engine taxiing for a takeoff.

Mark returned and said he'd left a message for Carol at the front desk. Then he observed his supposed woman-hating cat sitting on Katherine's lap. Mark remarked that he couldn't understand what had come over Bruiser. Katherine explained that she had a way with cats.

They had lunch in a quaint restaurant near the town's limits. At six p.m. they attended a reception—in Katherine's honor—at Mayor Ralph Newman's residence. There she met the mayor and his wife, the town's only physician and her husband, and a university professor who had written several books. Afterward, Mark drove Katherine to the city thirty miles away. They spent a few minutes at the mausoleum where Orvenia Colfax was interred, then had a quiet dinner in an Italian restaurant.

By eleven, when Mark dropped her off at the Little Tomato, Katherine was exhausted. She desperately wanted to curl up in bed—under the covers—because she was still chilled to the bone by the short walk from Mark's car to the front door of the bed and breakfast.

Once inside, Katherine hastened up the carpeted steps. She turned the key in her guest room lock and went inside. She immediately noticed a feather comforter draped over the wicker chair by the bed. She read out loud the note signed by Carol Lombard: "I apologize for the cold. Our furnace is doing the best it can, but when the temperature outdoors is ten degrees below zero, it's very difficult to keep an old house like this warm. I hope this feather comforter does the trick. The key to warmth is layers."

"Warmth in layers," Katherine huffed. A feather comforter and a heavy, quilted bedspread were already on the bed, she noted. She envisioned her body being crushed into the soft mattress by the tremendous weight of warmth in layers. Then she laughed and wondered if there were other twenty-six-year-old curmudgeons.

The wind started to howl outside and whip around the B&B, rattling the antique windows. Katherine opened the heavy draperies and brushed some of the frost off the glass. She pressed her nose against the glass and looked outside. It had just started to snow. She began to worry. She envisioned mountains of snow preventing her from ever leaving Erie. She feared it would take months to make it back to Manhattan. She would miss her meeting on Monday. She snapped out of her reverie. *I'm just tired*, she thought.

She threw on her fleece pajamas and rushed to the bathroom. She washed her face, brushed her teeth, then headed back to her room. She jumped under the covers and fell fast asleep—with the light dimly glowing overhead.

* * * *

She had been dreaming. She was eating a Zaro's carrot muffin at Grand Central Station during the early morning rush. Commuters scurried past. She studied the nameless faces, searching in vain for Gary DeSutter, who promised to meet her before work. Gary was late, as usual. She finished her muffin, then grew tired of standing, so she started to make her way through the throng of people when she heard a steady staccato sound.

"Iris," she murmured, still asleep. "Stop that."

The persistent staccato sound continued.

"Lilac, stop chattering at that damned pigeon and go back to sleep," she said sharply, sitting up in bed.

She sleepily looked around and realized she was still in Indiana. The intensity of the wind had picked up dramatically since she had gone to bed, but it seemed warmer. Something was hitting the glass of the window.

She darted out of bed and ran to the window. She pulled the heavy draperies back and looked outside. She was startled by the total transformation of the landscape—a thick white blanket of snow covered everything. *There must be a foot of snow out there*, she surmised. And, the sound—rapping insistently against the glass—was sleet.

Sleet, she thought. *Ice storm,* she worried.

She watched the sleet pelt the window glass until she imagined her feet were frostbitten. She leaped back into bed, and immediately jumped out again to check her watch—it was only four a.m. She decided to sleep for another hour or so and quickly lapsed into a deep slumber.

At eight o'clock there was a knock at the door.

"Ms. Kendall," a woman's voice said. "I've brought you coffee."

"One moment, please," Katherine said, jumping out of bed. She couldn't believe she had gone back to bed and managed to oversleep. She opened the door.

Carol Lombard stood outside, holding a tray with a coffeepot and a sweet roll. "You wanted me to wake you at eight?"

"Yes, thanks. Please come in," Katherine said.

The woman placed the tray on the dresser and then left.

Katherine's cell phone rang and she hurried to answer it. She glanced at the incoming number, then said, "I was just going to call you."

"I'm so tired," Colleen complained. "I don't think I slept a wink last night. I'll be so relieved when you get back. Actually, I'm just kidding. The cats have been great. I had to lock them out of the bedroom last night because the big one—"

"Scout?"

"Yeah, her. She tried to strangle me."

"That's how she sleeps at night."

"Oh. Anyway, they didn't appreciate it at all. They howled like banshees and carried on for hours. 'Twas a nightmare to behold. I finally got up and moved their cat bed out into the living room next to the radiator. They immediately curled up and went to sleep."

"Perfect."

"Hey listen, Katz, is there something wrong with your cell phone? Your boss called and left a voice mail on your home phone. I saw the machine blinking and thought I'd just leave it alone, and you could check it when you got home. But Scout jumped up and stepped on the button."

"Ah, my good girl," Katherine cooed.

"Anyway, Monica complained that you hadn't been checking your voice mail."

"It's the weekend, for pity sake," Katherine said.

"She canceled the meeting for tomorrow morning."

"She did what?" Katherine exclaimed in disbelief.

"She rescheduled it for Tuesday."

"Why didn't she tell me on Friday before I booked my flight?"

"That's why I called you. Now you can stay in Indiana for another day."

"But I already paid for the round-trip ticket," Katherine lamented. "It cost me a fortune the way it was. If I change the ticket it will cost more, so forget it. I'm coming back this evening. I'll text you as soon as I land. We could order Chinese and have it delivered. You can tell me all about the office thing you attended, and I can tell you all about my Indiana thing."

"Sounds good," Colleen laughed. "But I may not be at your apartment when you get back. I have tons of stuff to do at home."

"Okay, we'll play it by ear. Thanks so much for taking care of my kids. Bye."

Katherine ended the call and took a sip of coffee. *Awful*, she thought. *Carol must have warmed it up from yesterday*. She jumped into bed, leaned back on the pillow, and thought about the decision she had to make.

Katherine weighed the pros and cons. She thought about the beautiful little bundle of fur named Abigail. She thought about the huge pink house and the guaranteed income for the rest of her life. She commanded an excellent salary in Manhattan, but she'd paid the price: hardly any free time for herself. She was very close to being promoted to a manager position, which would require more work and absolutely no play.

Katherine wondered how her boss would react to her resignation. Would Monica be surprised? Angry? Would she dart to the phone and call her brother Gary? She wondered how much lead time a moving company needed to schedule a long-distance move.

She weighed the cons. She would be making a radical change—urban to rural. From the rush of the city, to the slow pace of the town. She didn't know anyone in the town. She would have to make new friends. She would miss Colleen terribly. There would be no more hailing a cab and rushing off to the cinema for an eleven o'clock show, or two o'clock in the morning pizza deliveries. The town of Erie seemed to shut down at nine in the evening, with the exception of a few restaurants and bars.

She had just signed a two-year lease on her apartment. She was comfortable there. Yes, the space was small, and the cats would probably love running up and down the stairs at her great aunt's home. *But, wait*, she thought. *That's a favorable-move-to-Indiana point.*

She wondered if there could ever be a personal relationship with Mark. She was very attracted to him. He was easy to be around, but he'd said that his cat was jealous of his women friends, so she automatically assumed he had a girlfriend. She wondered about his relationship with Carol Lombard.

Katherine got up and began to get dressed. She imagined shipping seltzer from the Big Apple to the Little Tomato. *Why would I want to do that*, she thought, daydreaming, when I can have it shipped to the pink house on Lincoln Street?

Chapter Four

The flight to LaGuardia was a roller-coaster ride of bumps, swoops and jolts. The pilot warned they would experience patches of choppy air, and advised passengers and flight attendants to keep on their seatbelts. The scheduled snack was canceled, and no beverages were served.

Katherine clutched the hand rests and felt her wrist muscles cramp. She vowed that if they landed safely in New York, she would not subject her cats to this experience of nerve-fraying fear, but would drive them to Indiana instead.

The plane landed with a heavy thud and raced down the short runway. Katherine looked out the window at the thick fog. Rain pelted the plane, which seemed to take forever to taxi to the main terminal. Once there, Katherine was annoyed at the turtle-like pace of fellow passengers in front of her, who were slowly removing their belongings from the overhead bins. Once off the plane and inside the terminal, Katherine decided she would spend the extra money and take a cab, instead of catching the regular express bus to Grand Central. She walked outside the building and stood in the cab queue. Fortunately, only two people were ahead of her.

Inside the cab, she couldn't find her seat belt and gave up trying. The cab driver wore a red Sikh turban and spoke little English. He floored the accelerator and swerved out onto Grand Central Parkway. On the Brooklyn-Queens Expressway, he veered in and out of lanes.

"Could you slow down," she shouted over traffic.

"What?" he said, turning around.

"Watch out," she warned.

"Oh! Ha, ha!" he said, nearly crashing into a service van.

Miraculously, they arrived in Manhattan. The reckless cabby pulled up to Katherine's apartment building and temporarily double-parked to let her out. *Thank God,* she thought, relieved to be alive outside her building.

She grabbed her carry-on and stepped out of the car, into a puddle deep enough to cover her shoes. "Just great," she said irritably, handing the driver the fare. "I'm not tipping you because I think you're a menace on the highway." She slammed the door. The driver said, "Oh! Ha, ha!" and peeled out into traffic, splashing the front of Katherine's coat.

When Mario, the doorman, observed the scene, he ran outside, and said dramatically, "Hey, Katz, do you want me to chase after him and get his medallion number?"

"Not thinkin' so," she said, watching the cab speed around the corner, screeching tires.

"Sorry about your coat." He hurried to the door and opened it for her.

"Oh, Mario," she said. "Thank you so much."

"You're welcome, Marie," he kidded, deliberately calling her by the wrong name.

"Mar-i-o," Katherine said, in her feigned Italian accent.

"I hope you don't mind my asking but . . ." He stopped.

"But, what?" Katherine asked.

"I saw a lot of your red-haired friend this weekend, going in and out, and I wanted to know if she's hooked up with anyone?"

"Colleen?" she asked nonchalantly.

"Do you think she'd go out with me?"

"What am I running here, a dating service?" she teased. "Why don't you ask her and see."

He hesitated, then said, "I was wondering if you would—"

"Test the waters," she finished. "Sure—for you, Mario—the world. Listen, buzz me in quick. I haven't seen my cats since Friday night. I miss them terribly."

He pressed the buzzer. "See you later, Marie," he said happily.

The elevator was resting on the first floor with its doors open. Katherine couldn't believe her good luck. Usually she had to wait several minutes for the next available car. She rushed into the elevator—not stopping to even check her mail—and pressed the twenty-second floor. The elevator shot up and opened the doors to her floor.

She couldn't believe her second stroke of good luck. Normally, the elevator went local and stopped on every floor. As the doors glided open, she heard the distinct feline cries of welcome—the loud waugh of Scout, and the yowl of Iris, but she didn't hear the me-yowl of Lilac. *That's odd*, she thought. She raced down the hall, imagining all sorts of catly horrors—Lilac trapped in the closet, or Lilac kidnapped and held for ransom. As Katherine ran, she called their names: Lilac . . . Scout . . . Iris.

Something's wrong, she worried. She turned the key in the upper lock, then struggled with the bottom lock. "Colleen," she called through the door. "Are you there?" There was no answer. She opened the door and fumbled for the light switch. "Waugh." "Yowl." The two seal-points crashed into her legs. "Owl," a hoarse voice said, nearby.

When Katherine spotted the lilac-point, she had to look twice. Lilac was moving her jaws but no sounds were coming from it. "Have you lost your voice?" she asked the meowless cat. Scout and Iris continued their caterwauling. "Quiet," she said, closing the door. Scout and Iris hiked up their tails and marched to the kitchen. Lilac began prancing and pacing in front of Katherine. "What's wrong with you?" she asked, setting down her carry-on.

Lilac bolted and raced down the hall, stopping outside Katherine's clothes closest. She reached up with her long, gray paws and tried to turn the doorknob, but the door wouldn't open.

Katherine said amused, "I bet your toy is in there, right? Your bear? You batted it in the closet and then Colleen shut the door. I forgot to tell her to never close the closet."

"Owl," Lilac said.

Katherine joined the cat outside the door. "This explains why you drove Colleen crazy with your serenade." She opened the closet door. Inside, on the floor, the bear was stuck inside one of her shoes.

Lilac flew inside and pounced on her prize—a three-inch teddy bear that was missing both an arm and a leg. With jaws of steel, she gripped the bear by the head and carried the toy into the living room. "Owl," she said in muffled thanks.

Katherine walked into the kitchen and found a note taped to the refrigerator. "Katz," it began. "It's 4:00. Gotta go. Fed cats. Heading for the Laundromat. Call me as soon as you get home."

She dialed Colleen's home number and Colleen's mother answered with her heavy Irish brogue. "Murphy residence," she said.

"Hello, Mrs. Murphy," Katherine said.

"Katz, is it you?"

"I just got home. Where's Colleen?"

"She's off to the Laundromat. You sound tired. Do you want me to take a message?"

"Yes, tell her: I'm home. I'm in love. And call me later."

"I'm glad you made it home safely. Should I be planning to bake your wedding cake soon?" she offered in obvious amusement.

"Oh, no. It's nothing like that. I wouldn't want to jinx anything."

"I'll give Colleen the message. Bye to you for now."

Katherine hung up the phone. Colleen's mom was like a mother to her. She always teased that she had four boys but needed a second girl. Katherine, with no living relatives, gladly volunteered.

"Waugh," Scout said, breaking Katherine's reverie.

Scout and Iris sat next to their dinner bowls and looked up pitifully.

"Are the royal Siamese hungry?"

"Yowl," Iris demanded.

Katherine opened a fresh can of tuna and first poured the juice in Scout's bowl. "Nectar of the gods, my darling," she said. Scout turned up her nose and ran into the living room. She put the rest of the juice in Iris's bowl. "Appetizer, dearest." Iris—with dramatic sweeps of her paw—tried to bury the bowl. "Fakers," Katherine said. "Lilac, catch of the day," she called enticingly to the living room.

Lilac streaked down the hall, disappearing into the bedroom, still clutching her bear.

Katherine transferred the tuna into a plastic bowl and put it in the refrigerator. The phone rang. She picked it up on the second ring.

"I've been trying to call you all weekend," the male voice complained.

"Gary?" Katherine said, surprised.

"Yes, *Gary*. Have you forgotten my voice? Did you think I'd died?"

"Possibly, but I wasn't sure," she said sarcastically. "Why are you calling?"

"I was wondering if you'd like to meet for drinks tomorrow night after work. I'm going to be in Midtown, and I thought it would be nice to sit back and have a nice chat about old times."

"Old times," she repeated. "Did Tamara dump you?"

There was a long pause, then he said, "How did you know?"

"Gut feeling. Gary, when I said it was over, I meant it. So please don't call me again—*ever!*" she stressed, hanging up the phone.

The phone rang immediately.

"Hello," she said angrily, thinking it was her ex-boyfriend calling again.

"It's me, Colleen. What's the matter?"

"Gary just called me. Can you believe the nerve?"

"What did he want?"

"To meet for drinks."

"Did you give him the name of that bar we used to go to that burned down last week? Since he lives out-of-town, he'd never know. When he got to the place, he'd realize you'd stood him up. Wouldn't it be a hoot?"

"Not really," Katherine said, feeling suddenly depressed.

"Don't let it get you down. Mum said you sounded so happy on the phone—tired, but happy. When's the wedding?"

"Wedding," Katherine said sharply, still fuming about Gary. "How about the wake?"

"No, not Gary. Mr. Lawyer. You said you were in love."

"In love with the cat," Katherine stressed.

"The cat," Colleen laughed. "What about the lawyer? Was he cute?"

"He was ninety-five and used a walker."

"For real?"

"No, just kidding."

"I have to dart back to the Laundromat. I just came home to get the fabric softener. My clothes are still cooking. Speaking of cooking, Chinese sounds great, but I must tend to the clothes. Want to meet for lunch tomorrow?"

"Sure. Cottage cheese and apple," Katherine teased. Colleen was always concerned about her weight.

"Very funny. How about meet me at Grand Central at 1:00 and we'll go from there to the Mexican place."

"Beef burrito sounds good. Meet you there," Katherine said, hanging up.

Katherine went into her bedroom and was surprised to see her computer turned on. Normally after so many minutes, a screensaver would pop up on the flat-screen monitor. If Colleen had used the PC, Katherine surmised, and she had left the apartment hours before, the computer should have been in sleep mode. Or, she thought, one of the cats walked across keyboard. That would wake up the PC. But they would have had to done it in the last half-hour. But now, not only was the computer active, but someone had done a Google search. The topic on-screen was toxic poisoning. Katherine stepped back, surprised. For a moment, the hair on the back of her neck stood up. She thought of the argument she overheard at her great aunt's house about the dangerous weed. Lilac came out from under the bed and tried to jump on the monitor, but instead fell back on the keyboard, which caused a series of beeping sounds.

"You little monkey," Katherine said. "Did you wake up the computer?" She picked up the Siamese and put her on the office chair.

Lilac tucked her paws underneath her, adjusted her body to maximum comfort, then squeezed her eyes.

Katherine pulled up a second chair.

"I'll fix you, my smart meezer." She leaned over and exited the search. She then logged onto her office email account and pulled up her messages. An array of junk mail appeared on the screen. She deleted those, and ignored the three messages from her boss. The one from Colleen was the same as the note taped on the refrigerator, but she was particularly interested in the email from Mark Dunn.

She opened it. "I enjoyed this weekend so much. I hope you've returned safely to NYC. You promised to give me an answer within forty-eight hours. Yes, I'm pressuring you. What may it be?"

"Indiana wants me," she said to Lilac, who was still resting on the office chair. "Scout . . . Iris," she called. She waited a few seconds, and then called them again. "Where are you guys?" she asked. When she didn't hear the pitter-patter of little feet, she had a good idea where they would be—basking in front of the radiator.

She pulled Lilac off the chair. The cat squawked, still hoarse from the ordeal of her incarcerated bear. She carried the cat into the living room where—sure enough—the other two cats were stretched out in front of the radiator. Scout was on her side with eyes closed; one fang showed under her curled upper lip. Iris was on her back with her eyes crossed slightly. Both were in total cat bliss.

"Don't sit so close to the radiator," she admonished. "You'll get toasted."

Iris got up, stretched, and then slinked over, collapsing on Katherine's foot. "Yowl," she said, and then yawned. "Waugh," Scout protested, not moving.

"Cats of mine, we're moving to Indiana," Katherine announced. "Tomorrow I'm giving my two-week notice. I have to schedule a time with the moving people. I'll do this and that, and oh yes, I must have the car serviced."

At the mention of car service, the cats' ears flew back in defensive mode. They didn't like these particular words. Car service generally meant a trip to the veterinarian, where they would be poked and prodded by a human with cold hands, and sometimes receive the dreaded shot. Scout uttered an emphatic waugh, which sounded almost like no. Iris squeezed her eyes, sauntered back to the radiator and began grooming her paw. Lilac struggled to get down—kicking Katherine with her hind legs as she catapulted onto the floor. "Owl," she cried, as she galloped out of the room.

"Scout votes no, Iris and Lilac vote yes."

By the time Katherine got back to her desk, Lilac had resumed her position on top of her chair. She leaned over and read the three remaining messages—written by her boss in her typical taskmaster tone—work, work, work. The corporation had downsized to the barest of staff, which meant those employees lucky enough to keep their jobs were unlucky enough to acquire several more. "I need to get a life," Katherine said to the sleeping cat.

Walking into the kitchen, she poured herself a glass of cabernet, then dialed the Indiana attorney's home number.

The phone rang twice. Katherine heard the sound of a phone being picked up, then dropped to the floor.

"Bruiser," Mark scolded. "Get away from that phone. Hello," he said into the receiver.

Katherine chuckled, "I see we have similar problems. Bruiser doesn't like the phone ringing either?"

"I'm so glad you called," Mark said. "How was your flight?"

"A total nightmare. Snow in Indiana. Fog and rain in New York. Choppy air in-between," she said. "My cab driver was from hell and he drove that way, too. I got drenched outside the apartment. Need I go on?" she added ruefully.

Mark laughed. "I think I get the picture."

"The reason I'm calling is I've made a decision."

"And does the decision involve a long-distance move?" he asked hopefully.

"Yes, it does."

"Wonderful. How soon can you get here?"

"By the end of the month. I'd very much appreciate if you'd contact your New York connection to begin whatever they have to do to get me out of my lease."

"I'll need your landlord's name and address."

"I'll email it to you."

"How are you getting out here?"

"I'll drive out by car. My car isn't the latest model, and in fact, it needs the brakes serviced, but I believe it will get my cats and me to Erie."

"Are you sure you don't want to fly?"

"Not after today's flight," she said adamantly.

"The mountains in Pennsylvania can be pretty difficult in the winter," he warned.

"No problem. Can we talk tomorrow? I'm really tired, and I've a big day ahead of me."

"Sure," he said. "I'll call you tomorrow night."

"Perfect," she said, hanging up.

* * * *

By one o'clock the next day, the rain had ended, but the sky remained cloudy. Katherine met Colleen at Grand Central, and they walked across the street to Flaming Fajitas, a Mexican restaurant.

As soon as they sat down, Katherine summoned the waiter. "Two margaritas on the rocks—"

Colleen interrupted, "Make mine frozen."

The waiter nodded, then headed to the bar.

Colleen asked, "Why are we drinking so early in the day?"

Katherine began, "I don't know about you, but I need a little pick-me-up before I go back to the office."

"Why?"

"I'm quitting my job at the end of next week."

"I'm so happy for you, Katz," Colleen said gleefully. "I'll miss you very much, but I know you'll find happiness out there in Eerieville."

"Erie," Katherine corrected.

"Just kidding."

The waiter came over and placed a basket of tortilla chips and a bowl of salsa on the table, then headed back to the bar.

Katherine picked up a chip, scooped up some salsa, then proceeded to spill the salsa down the front of her suit jacket. "Incredible," she said. "How do I always manage to do that?"

"You need seltzer," Colleen said. She motioned to the waiter, who appeared to be listening to their conversation. He nodded and returned with a can of sparkling water.

He opened the can and offered to help. Katherine brushed his hand away and said a polite "thank you." He winked, then went away.

"My dry cleaner is really going to miss my business when I move," Katherine mused, blotting the stain.

Colleen smirked and said, "I tried to get a hold of you this morning four times, but I kept getting your voice mail."

"I'm sorry I didn't call you back, but I've been on the phone all morning—scheduling two different moving companies to come over and give me a bid. One is coming tonight at 7:00, the other tomorrow at 3:00."

"Isn't your big meeting tomorrow?" Colleen asked, dipping into the salsa.

The waiter brought over two margaritas. "It's on the house," he said seductively.

Katherine looked at him curiously, then thanked him.

After he left, Colleen said, "He's in love."

"Oh, geez. He is not," Katherine said, then added, "The meeting is in the morning. I'll be finished by one o'clock. I'm going to try to take off tomorrow by two-thirty. After I meet with these moving people, I need to take my car in to be serviced."

"Why don't you just buy a new car?"

"I don't want to shell out the bucks until I know this inheritance thing is a done deal. Besides, until I'm residing in my great aunt's house, I get nothing."

"Wait a minute. I thought you were supposed to get thirty thousand bucks right off the bat?" Colleen questioned.

"No, my great aunt made it quite clear in her will that she wanted someone in the house minding her cat before any money is released from her estate."

The waiter returned, and Katherine and Colleen both ordered the beef burrito special. He winked at Katherine a second time.

When he was out of earshot, Katherine said, "Do you think that guy has something in his eye?"

"I think he has a crush," Colleen teased.

* * * *

Katherine returned to work and left a second voice mail for her out-of-office boss, requesting a time in the early afternoon when they could talk for a few minutes. She keyed in her resignation letter and edited it three times before she finally printed the final version. She was busy deleting email accounts from the main server—five employees had been terminated the previous week—when her boss returned to the office and immediately requested that they meet in the main conference room.

Katherine logged off the system and joined her boss in the nearby room. "Hello, Monica," Katherine said pleasantly to the middle-aged woman, who was sitting at the end of a long walnut table, sorting through a stack of papers.

"Please have a seat," Monica said quickly. "I hate to have to do this, but I have been instructed by upper management to advise you that your position here at Computer Net no longer exists."

"What? You've got to be kidding," Katherine said, startled.

"I'm very sorry. I realize this comes as a great shock, but we feel that your job is no longer crucial to the company's operations. As you are aware, with our merger with INET, we in the Manhattan office are going to focus more on selling our products. We'll hire outside consultants to do the training. Because you don't have experience as a marketing rep, we have no other choice but to eliminate your position."

"Why don't we cut the work-a-talk, mumbo jumbo crap, Monica? What you really mean to say is that Computer Net is firing me," Katherine said curtly. After a long pause, she added, "Is the company offering me a termination package?"

"Why, yes," Monica said, a little taken back by Katherine's abruptness. "I have a check here for one month's salary, plus three months' severance pay."

Katherine took the envelope but didn't open it. "Am I to report to work tomorrow?" Katherine asked coolly.

"No," Monica said hurriedly. "We'll have someone pack up your belongings, then hire a messenger to bring them over to you. Or we can ship it. Your choice." She hesitated, then stated, "We want you to leave ASAP."

"Wow. That's brutal," Katherine said bitterly. She opened the envelope to verify the check amount.

"Also, here's a packet of documents—insurance and 401K paperwork you'll need to fill out and send to headquarters. In addition, we'll need your company credit card, laptop computer, and security pass," Monica said, then added, "Thank you very much for your service. Please be advised that once you find a new position, I'll personally give you an excellent recommendation." She got up and started to leave.

"One moment," Katherine said. "Allow me two seconds to write the address where I want my belongings sent." She hurriedly wrote down her great aunt's Erie address.

"Erie, Indiana?" Monica asked cuttingly.

"Yes," Katherine said, securing the paycheck in the front pocket of her suit jacket. "Last week I inherited several million dollars, but this small, token amount shall help me in the interim." She picked up the packet of documents and left the conference room.

Monica stormed out of the room, past Katherine, and into her office, slamming the door. Monica's absence let Katherine cruise around the office one last time to say good-bye to those remaining employees who had not been "eliminated."

On the way out of the office, Rosemary called after her. "Ms. Kendall, I have a message for you."

Katherine walked to the reception desk.

Rosemary smiled and handed her a pink message slip. She'd written: "We'll miss you very much. Best of luck and keep in touch."

Katherine went behind the desk and hugged Rosemary. Then she made her way to the elevator bank. On her way down to the lobby, she thought, *I've been here four years and I never thought in a million years that my job would be eliminated.*

When she got home, she threw her coat on the sofa and walked over to the steam radiator. Scout was almost on top of it. The other two were nestled nearby. Katherine reached down and pulled Scout away from the heater; the cat looked up sleepily, then turned over on her back. Katherine went into her bedroom and began to change into casual clothes when she heard her cell phone ring in the next room. She rushed into the kitchen to extract it from her bag. "Hello," she said, cradling the phone in the crook of her neck.

"Hi, Katherine," Mark Dunn said.

"Katz," Katherine reminded.

"I have bad news."

"Make my day," Katherine countered.

"Mrs. Marston had a stroke today and is in the hospital."

"Stroke," Katherine said in disbelief.

"Her daughter found her on the back stairs. Apparently, she'd been lying there for several hours. The ambulance rushed her to a hospital in the city. She's in the Intensive Care Unit. I'll keep you posted on her condition."

"I'm terribly sorry, Mark."

"If you need to reach me in the evenings, I'll be staying in your great aunt's home for the rest of this week. I moved Bruiser over there this afternoon. Vivian's daughter, Patricia, is moving in this weekend, and will stay until you get here. Just call my cell or text me."

"My arrival will be sooner than I expected."

"How soon?" he asked, surprised.

Today is the fifth, she thought. "Next weekend—February 18th."

"I don't have my calendar in front of me. Is that on a Saturday or Sunday?"

"Late on Sunday. Listen, I'm meeting with a mover tonight. If I can get a rush job, there won't be a need for me to delay. My request is that Patricia stay in the house until the 17th."

"I'll let Patricia know. I'll also have Cokey move Vivian's belongings back to her apartment by then. I wish you'd reconsider, and fly to Indiana instead of driving," he said, changing the subject.

"No, that's okay. I'm going to drive."

"In the dead of winter? Seriously, my office can make all of your traveling arrangements," he stressed.

"That won't be necessary," she said. "I have to get my car to Indiana somehow, and I think the cats will be more comfortable in the car instead of some cold luggage bay in a jet."

"Well, at least allow me to send you a map," he offered. "I can email you the best route."

"I have GPS. But thanks anyway."

"No problem."

"Oh, yes, before I hang up. First, I'll pick Abigail up on the nineteenth. Could you notify Dr. Sonny? And, second, I want a locksmith to change every exterior lock on the house."

"Why?" Mark asked quizzically.

"I'm a native New Yorker, and we believe in security. I'm not sure how many keys my great aunt gave to her employees. To be safe, I want to know I'm the only one in possession of the keys."

"I understand," he said. "I'll schedule a locksmith right away."

"Thanks," she said. "I'm very sorry about Mrs. Marston."

"I'll call you tomorrow," he said.

Katherine pressed the END button and immediately punched in Colleen's home number. One of Colleen's brothers answered. "Murphy's," he said.

"Jimmy, Jacky, Joey or Johnnie?" she inquired.

"It's Jacky. Is this Katz?"

"Yes, has Colleen gotten home from work yet?"

"No, she's off to Paddy's Pub with that guy you fixed her up with."

"I didn't fix her up with any guy. What are you talking about?"

"Yes, you did," he argued. "His name is Mario and he works in your building."

"Oh, *that* Mario. Wow. That was fast. Oh, listen Jacky, I'll just call her on her cell."

Mario, she thought. *Fast worker.*

She started to call Colleen, but decided to text her instead. "Have one on me!" She'd tell her the doom-and-gloom stories tomorrow.

Chapter Five

Katherine signed the last page on the bill of lading and watched the delivery man load three remaining boxes onto a hand truck, then push it through the apartment doorway. Lilac made a mad dash to escape, but Katherine caught her. "Trying to run away from home?" she asked the errant cat. "Me-yowl," Lilac screeched. She squirmed free and raced down the hall into the living room. The deliveryman, who had complained of being allergic to cats, sneezed for the hundredth time, then disappeared down the hall toward the elevator bank. Katherine was sure he was anxious to get away from three shedding felines.

Katherine had decided to send her clothing and other personal items to Indiana by a parcel delivery service, and leave behind her furniture and other bulky items for now. Colleen and her brother Jacky had agreed to sublet the apartment. Jacky was a carpenter and was going to convert the one-bedroom flat into a two-bedroom unit by partitioning the living room. A short-term sublet to her friends was ideal for Katherine, because she wouldn't have to give up the apartment in the event the Indiana situation didn't work out.

Katherine's patience had been tested by the cats, who endeavored to help assemble and pack twenty boxes. Scout kept carrying off the roll of tape, Iris kept jumping in and out of boxes, and Lilac kept hiding in the box that was currently being packed. Whenever Katherine had enough of their shenanigans, she'd lock them in the bedroom. They would be quiet for a few minutes, until they realized they were being excluded from an activity worthy of their assistance, and then collectively launch into a wailing session that threatened to violate the city noise ordinance. Katherine could tolerate their high-pitched shrieks for only a few minutes before freeing them to resume their meddling all over again. To make matters worse, Lilac kept burying her bear in each unsealed box, darting off to get into further mischief, then returning to reclaim the toy after Katherine had fastened the box with tape. She whined incessantly until Katherine unsealed the box and rescued the bear.

The cats seemed to know a change was in their future, because they increased their restless exploration and became more talkative. None of the cats except Scout had ever been on an extended road trip before, and Scout may or may not have had a fond memory of her traveling with Magic Harry. The most time any of them had recently spent in a car was less than an hour, which was the time it took to drive to the vet's office in lower Manhattan. Now Katherine was about to embark on a road trip that would take at least eight or nine hours the first day, and about the same on the next day.

Colleen had readily agreed to ride with Katherine to Indiana, then fly back to Queens a week later. During that week, Colleen's four brothers volunteered to move her clothing and other personal belongings into Katherine's apartment, so when she returned, she would be able to instantly set up shop. Mario, the doorman, was thrilled when he learned Colleen was subletting the apartment. In his amorous effort to further ingratiate himself with Colleen, he enlisted his help to make sure the move was successful—at least on his end, which was opening and shutting the front lobby security door.

When Mario heard Colleen would pick up Katherine's car so she could finish packing, he volunteered to accompany her to the parking garage. He counted his lucky stars that he arrived early for his shift, and had literally run into his Irish heartthrob at six-thirty in the morning as she was headed out the building, en route to the parking garage.

Katherine decided to wait until Mario and Colleen returned before she dared corral the cats. She knew from past experience that collecting the cats would be relatively easy compared to enticing them into their traveling cage, which they associated with trips to the vet. She bought a large-size dog carrier to squeeze into the back seat. The cats often snuggled up together during naps and sleep time, and Katherine assumed one large carrier would be more agreeable to the picky Siamese than three separate cages.

That was Katherine's first mistake. The second mistake was the larger carrier's great weight, once all the cats were in it. It took two people to carry it, and the carrier was difficult to wedge in the back seat.

Katherine placed two of her fluffiest towels on the carrier floor. Scout immediately jumped in, walked around the perimeter, sniffed, then flopped down into a tranquil repose. *Perfect,* she thought. Iris strolled in and plopped down next to Scout. *Amazing,* she reflected. She attempted to quickly close the steel grate door, but it squeaked loudly on its hinges and terrified the sensitive seal-points, who bounded out of the carrier, scurried into the bedroom, and darted under the bed. "Waugh," Scout scolded. "Yowl," Iris added.

Lilac strolled out of the kitchen, carrying her bear. She jumped on top of the carrier and dropped the stuffed toy. "Lilac, my little darling," Katherine said soothingly. The very moment she grasped Lilac, the doorbell buzzed, which caused the frightened feline to break free of Katherine's grip and rocket into the next room, joining Scout and Iris beneath the bed.

Katherine ran down the hall to open the door. Mario stood outside.

"Hey, Marie," he teased. "Colleen's down on the street, double-parked. She says I'm to help you carry your cats."

"Oh Mario, thank you so much, but first I have to herd my kids into their traveling carrier."

"Can I help?"

"I'm good. Just stay here for a minute. I'll coax them into the carrier, and then we can take them downstairs."

The telephone rang in the kitchen. Racing down the hall, Katherine answered the phone on the third ring.

"Leaving without saying good-bye?" The voice on the other end had a sarcastic tone.

"I can't talk now, Gary," Katherine lied. "Can I call you later?"

"Katz, I want to see you before you leave."

"Not interested."

"Just hear me out. Moni told me your news."

"Monica had no right to do that," Katherine fumed.

"I guess Moni's loyalties lie with the family, not the job."

"What do you want?" she asked bitterly.

"Indiana," he said cynically. "I can see you and the cats staring out a large picture window at cows in the meadow, chewing their cud."

"Gary, that's one of your big-time limitations," she began. "When you fly on business from the East Coast to the West Coast, you never stop and check out the in-between."

"Maybe I'll do that someday," he suggested.

"Not in your lifetime," she said. "This is good-bye. Have a nice life. And," she said firmly, "Never—ever—call me again!" She slammed the receiver down so forcibly that the phone fell off the table.

"Everything okay, Marie?" Mario asked earnestly, still standing at the front door.

Katherine took a deep breath and walked into the hallway, "Yes, Mario. I'm sorry you had to hear that. I need to get my cats in the carrier before Colleen gets a parking ticket." She walked into the bedroom, spouting wonderful compliments about the cats' good looks. She kneeled down and looked under the bed. She found Iris's cosmetic brush stash, but no cats.

"Where are you guys?" She went into the living room and was surprised to see three Siamese inside the carrier. Scout and Iris formed two compact bundles, sitting side-by-side and looking up at her with slanted, blue eyes. Lilac was nestled in the corner with her paw on the bear. Katherine didn't waste any time on a second glance, and hurriedly closed the metal door.

"Good girls," she cooed, "Okay, Mario. Mission accomplished. If you carry the cats, I'll get my bag and keys to lock up."

"Sure, Marie." He hurried down the hall, leaned down to pick up the carrier, and gazed inside. He made a kissing sound and said, "*Buon giorno*. What beautiful cats." Iris hissed.

"Did I say something wrong?" he asked.

"Iris is having a bad fur day," Katherine assured him.

She sadly said good-bye to her apartment and followed Mario down to the street. While Colleen sat behind the wheel, Mario and Katherine tried to push the large carrier through the door and onto the back seat.

"I think it's stuck," Katherine said worriedly. For a moment, she was terrified it wouldn't fit.

"It has to fit," Colleen noted. "We brought it here from the pet store."

With one final push, the carrier fit snugly through the door and settled onto the back seat. The cats huddled by the metal door and looked forlornly out the opening. Katherine leaned over and placed a small litter box behind the driver's seat.

"Say good-bye to New York," Colleen said.

The cats were unusually quiet.

"Quiet before the storm," Katherine muttered under her breath.

Colleen jumped out of the car and ran around to the passenger side.

"What are you doing?" Katherine asked, perplexed.

"I don't want to drive until we're out of the city."

"Oh, that's okay. I'll drive the first shift." Katherine hugged Mario and thanked him before she got into the car. Mario smiled, then winked at Colleen. "See you in a week," he said, beaming.

"Maybe," Colleen said mischievously.

"*Ciao*," he said to the cats.

"Me-yowl," Lilac belted hungrily.

"Not chow, honey," Katherine said.

"Oops," Mario laughed. "*Arrivederci!*"

Katherine placed her GPS on the dash, put the car in gear, and moved into traffic. Within two blocks, all hell broke loose in the carrier. For a large carrier that had previously been—with utmost difficulty—wedged in the back seat, it was now being rocked back and forth by Scout, who was having a complete cat fit. "Waugh," she screamed, kicking the side of the carrier. Iris yowled. Iris hissed. Lilac began whining. Scout kept on kicking like a kangaroo in some sort of crazed feline tantrum.

"Pull over. Pull over," Colleen shouted, looking back at the mayhem. "They're killing each other. I think that GPS lady is making them crazy."

"Make a left on Baxter Street," the machine said.

"Where the hell is that?" Katherine asked.

"Baxter Street," the machine repeated.

"Oh, turn that thing off," Colleen implored.

"Okay, okay," Katherine said, trying to turn down the device's volume with one hand. She crossed three lanes before she could find a spot to double-park. By now, Iris was in a rage and was pummeling Lilac, who was cowering in the corner, whimpering.

The GPS droned on, "Recalculating."

"I can't get her to shut up." Finally, Katherine tapped the off switch. "We've got to get Scout out of there."

"But we don't have a cage for her," Colleen said.

"She'll have to ride outside the cage."

Katherine got out of the car and ran to the passenger side. She partially climbed in the back seat and struggled to open the carrier's metal door. She extracted the hysterical Scout and held her to her chest, while Colleen reached around Katherine and shut the metal door. Iris gave out one more hiss before settling down. She immediately began to groom the terrified Lilac. Katherine held Scout close and cooed to her reassuringly. A group of homeless people stood nearby observing the scene. "Nice fruit bat," one of them said.

"Katz, we better go," Colleen said. "There's a traffic cop on the corner writing tickets."

Katherine set Scout down on top of the carrier and hurriedly shut the car door. Colleen slid back into her seat and Katherine resumed her driving position. She pulled out a piece of paper from her bag. "I'm going to follow the directions Mark sent me. No more GPS lady."

"Sounds like a plan."

Scout jumped to the back windowsill and sat like an Egyptian sphinx, staring at the traffic. She cried an incessant string of variations on "waugh" from "whoa" to "mir-waugh" to "ma-waugh" until the car had crossed the toll bridge between New Jersey and Pennsylvania. Then she quieted down and went to sleep. Meanwhile, the other two cats were snuggled in a fur ball, fast asleep. Lilac's paw was twitching.

"I think the little darlings are asleep," Katherine whispered.

"Waugh," Scout protested weakly, and then fell back to sleep.

"My neck hurts from checking," Colleen complained. "Are we there yet? I'm hungry. I need a spot of tea. Can we stop so I can go to the bat-room?"

"Bathroom," Katherine chuckled at her friend's pronunciation.

They drove on for another hour before stopping at a fast food restaurant. Katherine was afraid someone would break into the car and steal the Siamese, so she stayed in the car while Colleen went inside.

"Don't they need to go to the cat-room?" Colleen asked, returning to the car.

"They'll scream like banshees when they need to use the litter box, I'm sure," Katherine said. "But, just in case I'm going to leave this metal door open."

Iris and Lilac continued sleeping.

"I think the car motion has anesthetized them," Colleen joked.

Colleen traded seats with Katherine and began driving. They agreed to relieve each other every two hours. The car was getting excellent gas mileage, so they didn't have to stop for gas frequently.

Five hours into Pennsylvania, Katherine was behind the wheel. Scout had moved from the rear window ledge to inside the carrier. The three cats formed a tight circle; Scout was snoring intermittently.

"Where are we staying?" Colleen asked in reference to their overnight accommodations.

"Akron."

"Akron?" she asked. "Where's that?"

"It's in Ohio. We're so lucky it hasn't snowed."

Colleen put up her hand as if to ward off an enemy attacker. "Don't say that. You've just jinxed the trip. Now it's sure to snow."

"I watched the Weather Channel. Snow isn't in the forecast."

A few minutes later, flurries filled the air.

"Well, then, what are those things? See?" Colleen said, pointing. "It's snowing."

"That's just a little dusting from off Lake Erie."

The snowfall began to increase in intensity. It was accumulating quickly on the highway. Semi-trucks and cars began traveling at a snail's pace. The windshield wipers had difficulty keeping the heavy wet snowflakes off the glass. Outside the car, the landscape appeared surreal as the snow lent a soft and pendulous shape to every limb, tree, boulder and guardrail.

"Now what are we going to do?" Colleen asked nervously. "We'll never make it to Acorn doing forty miles per hour."

"Akron," Katherine corrected. "I think you're right. If this keeps up, I think we should find a motel and order room service."

"What if the motel doesn't allow pets?"

"We'll look for the Vacationer's Paradise chain. I checked. They allow cats and small dogs. Be on the lookout for a sign."

"That will be difficult, considering the fact it's snowing to beat the band, and I'm as blind as a bat."

Gusts of wind buffeted the little car. The cats woke up and began to cry. Lilac, who had been silent for most of the trip, began to me-yowl loudly.

"Colleen, reach back there and pick her up. You're going to have to hold her."

"Look, Miss Katz, I said I'd help you move to Indiana, but I don't remember saying anything about holding cats."

Lilac continued howling until Colleen couldn't stand it any longer. She flung herself over the seat and pulled Lilac out. She sat the startled cat on her lap. Lilac immediately quieted and began to purr noisily.

"I bet they're tired," Katherine said, slowing the car to thirty miles per hour.

The snow was flying straight at the windshield, so Katherine could barely see through it.

Colleen spotted a motel advertisement on a lighted billboard, and they pulled off at the next exit. After driving several miles, they found the motel. Unfortunately, other weary travelers shared the same notion, and had quickly filled the motel's vacancies. The manager was very apologetic and said, "Our Internet service is down, probably because of the storm. Let me call ahead to the next motel, which is forty miles away." He lifted the receiver and punched in the number. He spoke for a few seconds, then gazed at the fatigued travelers. "One room is available."

"But I wanted my own room," Colleen protested, not wanting to sleep in the same room with the rowdy cats.

"I'm sorry, ma'am," the manager said. "This is the last room up the road, but it's got double beds, so you'll at least have your own bed."

"Book it," Katherine said, almost shouting. She quickly wrote her name and number on a slip of paper and handed it to him.

"Consider it done," the manager replied.

"And thanks so much," the women said, rushing out the door. They got back into the car and brushed the snow off their coats. Scout had returned to the back-window ledge and was watching the snowflakes. She was trying to bat them with her paw. Iris and Lilac joined her in the back.

Katherine drove back to the interstate.

"You know, you could have saved ninety bucks and not bought that dog carrier," Colleen noted.

"Yes, but it will help when we have to take them inside the motel."

They drove the distance to the motel in silence. Once there, Colleen jumped out, slammed the door, and ran through the snow to the front office, while Katherine found a parking spot nearby. She leaned over the seat and tried to capture each one of the reluctant cats to put them back into the carrier. They moved further back on the back-window ledge.

"Come on, Scout," she coaxed. "I can't carry you outside. You'll get wet in the snow."

"Waugh," Scout wailed, scooting farther from Katherine's reach.

Iris and Lilac jumped back inside the carrier. "Good girls," Katherine praised.

Colleen returned and tapped on the glass. "Is it safe to come in?" she asked.

"Yes, but be quick about it."

"Our room is in the back on the first floor—number 23," Colleen said, climbing in.

Once inside the car, Katherine turned to Colleen and said, "Got a problem here. I can't get Scout inside the carrier, so I'll let you open the door to our room and then I'll carry her inside."

"If you think so," Colleen said worriedly.

Katherine parked and Colleen flew out of the car to open the motel room door. Katherine climbed over the seat and snatched Scout, who shrieked in resistance. After she skinned her knee getting out of the car, Katherine hurried into the room—with the struggling cat in her arms—and locked Scout in the bathroom.

"Scout, I'll have to wipe you off later," she called through the door. She turned to Colleen. "Let's bring the others in now."

Katherine and Colleen struggled with the carrier, but managed to maneuver it from the back seat. The snowflakes seemed wetter and clumped on top of the cage. Iris and Lilac shifted to the back of the carrier. Inside the room, Katherine let the two cats out, then went into the bathroom to dry Scout. Scout surprised Katherine by licking her on the nose. "Ingrate," Katherine scolded. "Waugh," Scout answered, licking her again.

Colleen called from the next room. "There's a card on the desk with the names of nearby restaurants. Believe it or not, there's an Irish pub close by."

"Woo hoo," Katherine said, joining her. "Let's get the cats situated, and then we'll check out the restaurant. I'm hungry for fish and chips."

"Fish and chips and a *pint*," Colleen added.

They returned to the car and found the bag with the cat food and drinking bowl. Katherine tucked it under her arm while she reached for the GPS.

"That thing is so annoying. Why don't you just leave it in the car. Maybe someone will steal it," Colleen quipped.

"Very funny. Could you get the litter box?"

"I guess."

Back in the room, they discovered the cats busily sniffing every inch of the space. Katherine placed the litter box in the bathroom. She poured spring water into their cat bowl, opened a can of premium cat food, and dished out three portions. The cats were more interested in getting drinks of water than the food.

"I think they're okay now," she said. "I really hate to go back out in this weather, but I'm famished."

"I'm absolutely starving," Colleen added.

The two left the room and drove to Irish pub. They sat at the bar and shared a large order of fish and chips. After they finished eating, Katherine texted Mark and keyed in a brief message: Staying in Clarion, PA. Snowstorm. Call or text me."

"Okay, let's just settle up and go back to the room," Colleen suggested.

"Excellent idea. I'm exhausted."

They paid their tabs and returned to the motel. As soon as they stepped through the door, Katherine's cell phone rang. One of the cats growled from under the bed.

Katherine quickly put the phone to her ear. "Hello."

"Hey, it's Mark. Snowstorm, huh?"

"We came upon a nasty storm in Pennsylvania and decided to check into a motel earlier than intended. I'm not sure how far Akron is from Clarion. I'd look it up, but we don't have Wi-Fi here."

"Hang on. I'll look it up on my map app." In a few seconds, he said, "You're about two hours from Akron. What's the weather doing now?"

"Just a sec," Katherine said, moving the curtains aside. "It's still snowing, but not quite as hard."

"Do you think you'll be able to travel tomorrow?"

"I'm optimistic. We're certainly going to try. I'm not sure what time we'll get to Erie. We plan on driving straight through."

"When you get close to Erie, call me so I can make sure I'm at the house."

"What if it's really late?"

"Not a big deal," he said. "Drive safely. I'll talk to you later. Bye."

Katherine set the phone down on the nightstand, then crawled onto the bed. "Well, I'm going to call it a day."

"Oh, does that mean I get the bat-room first," Colleen teased, climbing on top the other bed.

"Sure."

"Make sure those furry creatures of yours stay off of my bed." Colleen pulled the sheet over her head and feigned snoring. Lilac observed the lump and sneaked up onto the bed. She flattened into a stalking pose, raised her rump slightly, and wiggled it. Before Katherine could react, Lilac pounced on the unsuspecting Colleen. Colleen shot up out of the bed and screamed. Lilac scampered into the bathroom.

"Bad cat," Katherine scolded mildly.

"I knew I needed my own room," Colleen protested.

"She'll settle down in a while," Katherine said, then added facetiously, "But wait until the others come out."

"What?" Colleen said startled, getting up and walking to the bathroom.

"Just kidding."

* * * *

A shaft of sunlight fell through the opening between the curtains. Scout and Iris vied for a position on the narrow ledge. Scout fell from the window and scraped the wallpaper with her back claws. Katherine woke up.

"What time is it?" she shouted, nearly falling out of bed.

The covered lump in the next bed moved slightly and said sleepily, "I don't know."

Katherine grabbed her watch off the nightstand. "It's nine o'clock!"

"Why didn't the alarm go off?"

"Because the clock has gone missing."

"What?" Colleen asked, sitting up and wiping her eyes.

"I bet I know which one carried it away." Katherine looked suspiciously at Lilac, who was now taking her turn to jump onto the windowsill.

"The sun's shining. That must mean it stopped snowing."

"That's a good sign. We better get dressed. I vote we skip breakfast and eat a big lunch somewhere down the highway."

"Good idea."

The two hurriedly got ready. While Colleen showered, Katherine fed the cats, who ate heartily. "Good girls," she complimented.

When the time came to check out and put the cats into the dog carrier, Katherine said to Colleen. "You pick up L-i-l-a-c."

"Why are you spelling?"

"Because she associates "pick up" and her name to mean a trip to the V-e-t. Trust me, she'll be the first one to bolt, and then we'll never catch her. Hold her tight while I get I-r-i-s."

Total pandemonium broke out. The three Siamese streaked throughout the room, catapulting off of walls and jumping over beds until Katherine tackled Iris and Colleen caught Scout. Lilac rocketed under one bed, and lodged herself in the far recesses of the box spring's lining.

"Great," Katherine said in exasperation, putting Iris gently in the carrier and partially closing the door. Colleen handed Scout to her. "Waugh," Scout complained, trying to squirm away. Katherine put the struggling cat next to Iris and closed the metal door.

"How are we going to get Lilac out of there without ripping off the lining?" Colleen moaned.

"Where's Lilac's toy? Do you see her bear?"

Katherine and Colleen looked around the room. "There it is," Colleen said, picking the toy off the foot of her bed.

"I have a plan. We'll crawl under the bed and you'll hold the bear up to the opening in the lining. I'll be poised, ready to catch Lilac."

"Listen to this one," Colleen said incredulously. "Have you gone crazy? There might be creepy crawlies under there."

"Here, take the bear."

"For the love of Mary," Colleen protested, snatching the bear and getting down on her knees. She partially slid under the bed. "Ah-choo," she sneezed. "I found the clock."

"That's a relief," Katherine said joining her. "Now put the bear up where Lilac can see it and say, Qweek! Qweek!"

"Squeak, squeak," Colleen said in a monotone voice.

"No, not 'squeak.' Qweek! Qweek!" Katherine corrected. "It's a game we play."

Both women began saying "Qweek! Qweek!" Lilac hesitated for a moment, then lunged out the hole and grabbed the bear. Katherine seized Lilac and placed both the cat and the bear into the carrier.

* * * *

The rain pelted the small car as it headed south on Indiana State Highway 28. Katherine struggled to see the road through the dense fog and pounding rain. The squeaking and scraping of the cracked, aged windshield wipers had so frightened the cats, they had given up crying and now lay huddled in the far corner of the carrier.

"'Tis a nightmare to behold," Colleen said. "Do you realize it started raining on the Indiana-Ohio border, and it hasn't stopped since?"

"This is the worse drive I've ever done," Katherine said wearily.

"It snowed to beat the band in Pennsylvania," Colleen declared. "And now this wretched rain in Indiana. I hope this isn't an omen," she finished.

"Omen?" Katherine asked skeptically. "I don't believe in such nonsense. Maybe Mark was right and we should have flown."

"Shoulda, coulda," Colleen laughed. "But we didn't. At least we're almost there. That sign a while back said Erie was only nine miles away. What did Mark say when you called him?"

"He said he was relieved that we'd finally made it, and he's waiting for us at the house."

"Hey, look," Colleen said excitedly. "There's a sign for Erie."

"Woo hoo! This is the town limit. There's the Red House restaurant. I had lunch there."

The cats began meowing loudly. Katherine slowed down and said, "Help me look for Lincoln Street."

"Jackson Street . . . Washington Street . . . ," Colleen said as they drove by. "Here it is. Turn, turn."

Katherine split off the highway and began squinting for house numbers. "Look for 512."

Colleen cupped her face to the passenger side window, "It's so dark here. I can't see anything."

"There it is." Katherine stepped on the brake and did a complete stop in the middle of the street.

The house loomed like a pink giant. Every light had been turned on in the house, as well as the two outside lampposts. Katherine pulled into the driveway and parked under the covered carport. Mark's Honda was parked several feet away. The cats became unusually quiet.

"We're here, kids."

"Incredible. This house is huge," Colleen said, gathering her handbag and getting out of the car.

Mark opened the side door and bounded down the steps. "Welcome home," he said, smiling.

"Hello," Katherine said, as she began to unwedge the carrier from the back seat.

"I'll help you with that," he offered.

They transported the carrier up the stairs while Colleen held the door. They shuffled inside and positioned the carrier on the floor in the dining room. The cats began to move about anxiously. "Waugh," Scout protested.

"What beautiful Siamese," Mark admired.

"We should put them in the room where I'll be sleeping tonight as soon as possible—wherever that room may be," Katherine said.

"Patricia made up your great aunt's room. If you remember from the grand tour, it's the largest bedroom in the house," Mark explained. He turned to Colleen and said, "Your room is down the hall."

"Oh, I'm sorry," Katherine said. "Mark Dunn, this is my friend, Colleen Murphy."

"I'm pleased to meet you," he said, extending his hand.

Colleen shook it. When Mark turned to pick up the cat carrier, she winked her approval to Katherine.

Katherine mouthed the words, "Stop it."

"I think I can manage this alone," he said lifting the carrier.

"Waugh," Scout complained. "Me-Yowl," Lilac shrieked. "Yowl," Iris added.

"Scout, stop jumping," Katherine said, looking through the metal door. "You're stepping on Iris." Iris hissed. Scout boxed her on the ears. Lilac hovered in the corner.

Mark walked into the atrium and struggled with the dog carrier. The cats kept shifting from side to side, which made it difficult to hold level. "I lied," he said sheepishly. "Do you mind giving me a hand?"

Katherine grabbed the end of the carrier and peered in the cage. "I said stop it," she reprimanded the cats.

Colleen remained in the atrium, awestruck at the splendor of the house. "This house is a palace!"

"Ms. Murphy," Katherine called halfway up the stairs. "Don't you want to see your room?"

Colleen bounced up behind them. "My own room," she said playfully.

"We're punch drunk from the drive," Katherine explained to Mark. "Which way do we go, left or right? This house is so big, I forgot which room was my great aunt's."

"First door on the left."

They carried the cats into the bedroom and set the carrier down on the red Oriental carpet.

"Where's my room?" Colleen asked.

"Fourth door down the hall on the left—at the very end," Mark answered, and then to Katherine, "Listen, I hope you don't mind, but I set up the cat stuff in here. I assumed you'd want to keep them locked up with you the first night."

Katherine looked around and observed the litter box in the corner. "Thanks," she said. Near the armoire were several empty bowls for food, and a bowl of water. She closed the door, bent down, and opened the carrier door. "Come out and see your new home."

Scout was the first to leap out. She was followed by a reluctant Iris and skittish Lilac. Immediately, the three of them began sniffing various articles in the room. Lilac had found an unappealing odor—undetectable to the human nose—under the nightstand. She scrunched up her face and pulled her lips back to expose her fangs. Iris had discovered an imaginary spot on the rug and was busy burying it with wide sweeps of her paws. Scout had already opened the closet door and was inside investigating.

"Allow me to unload your car," Mark offered.

"Thanks," Katherine said, smiling.

They heard a scream, and then the sound of someone running down the hall.

"Colleen!" Katherine shouted.

Lilac and Iris shot under the bed. Iris growled. Scout dashed out of the closet and hurtled toward the door as Mark yanked it open.

"Oh, no you don't," Katherine said, snatching her.

Mark and Katherine rushed into the hall. Colleen was standing near the landing, holding something in her hand.

"Are you okay?" Katherine asked.

"I'm good. I'm sorry I screamed. I thought I'd broken it," she said, holding up a black instrument.

"Is that your ghost hunting gizmo?"

"Yes, it's new. The latest model," she said excitedly. "It's a K2 EMF meter. It detects spikes in electromagnetic energy."

"So, what are you doing with it now?" Mark asked, perplexed.

"I thought I saw someone pass by my door."

Katherine said to Mark, "Is there anyone else in the house?"

"No," he said firmly. "But I'd better take a look to make sure." He sprinted down the stairs two at a time.

"Was it a man or woman?" Katherine asked.

"Just a dark shape. I had my back turned, rummaging in my bag, when I felt someone looking at me. When I turned around, I saw this black shape—like a dark fog. I rushed into the hall but didn't see anything, so I got my meter out. Katz, for a moment the red light came on."

"So? What does that mean?"

"It means this house may have a spirit," Colleen said eagerly.

"Okay, definitely both of us need to get some sleep," Katherine suggested.

Mark returned. "I didn't find anyone downstairs, but let me have a look up here." He searched four of the five bedrooms, excluding Katherine's.

"Have all the exterior locks been changed?" she asked.

"Yes. In fact, I want to give you your keys." He reached in his pocket and pulled out a key ring. "Each key is individually labeled. The writing is small, but readable."

"Yeah, with an electron microscope," she said lightly.

"Are you okay?" Mark asked Colleen.

"I'm just tired and seeing things," Colleen said drowsily. "I have a few bags in the car. I think I'll fetch them and then call it a night."

"Good idea," Katherine said. "Me, too."

"I'll help you," Mark said.

The three went out to the car and unloaded it. After several trips they emptied the car. Colleen went upstairs to her room, while Katherine followed Mark into the kitchen. She saw two food trays on the red Formica and chrome table. "You made food for us? How thoughtful."

"Just a few things to make sandwiches. Are you hungry?"

"Yes, famished, but I'm too tired to eat."

"I'd better put it away before it spoils," he said, putting the sandwich tray into the empty refrigerator.

"What about this tray?" Katherine asked.

"I think we can leave it out. Those are Patricia's famous poppy seed muffins."

"That was very kind of her."

"I'm so glad you made it safely," he said, getting serious. "I hope you'll be very happy."

"Thanks, I plan on it."

They both were startled by the sound of a heavy object crashing on the floor above them.

"What room is that?" Katherine asked, dashing into the dining room.

"Sounds like Colleen's," Mark said, passing her and bounding up the stairs.

Katherine quickly followed him. "Colleen," she shouted.

"False alarm," Colleen said, rounding the corner of the upstairs hallway. In her hand, she was holding the broken base of a hurricane lamp. "I'm so sorry, but I seem to have caught the lamp on my sleeve, and before I could set it right, it fell to the floor. I'm afraid I've made a terrible mess. There's glass all over the floor."

"You gave us a fright," Katherine said, holding her heart. "I thought the dark shape had got you," she teased.

"I'll take care of it," Mark said, disappearing into another room, returning with a broom and dustpan.

"'Tis my mess," Colleen said firmly, taking the broom from his hands. "But thank you kindly for offering."

He handed it to her. "It was nice meeting you." He turned to Katherine. "I'll be going now."

"I'll walk you to the door," she said.

They walked down the stairs together. In the atrium, he said, "I'll be by around eleven to pick you up and go to Dr. Sonny's to fetch Abigail. I also need you to sign some papers."

"Papers?" Katherine asked inquisitively.

"A receipt for the initial distribution of money from Orvenia's estate."

"Could we go to a bank, as well? If you have appointments scheduled, I can go on my own."

"I have one appointment in the morning, but after eleven I'm officially taking the day off. I have a surprise to show you before I leave," he said changing the subject. "Stay right there." He opened one of the pocket doors to the living room, then announced, "Okay, you can come in now."

Katherine went in and immediately noticed her great aunt's portrait hanging to the left of the fireplace. "Oh, this is wonderful. Thank you so much."

"My pleasure. Now, I truly must go."

"See you tomorrow," she called after him. She opened the door leading to the covered carport.

"Lock up behind me," he said as he left.

"Thanks for everything."

He winked, then hurried down the steps.

Katherine walked from room to room, checking the locks on windows and doors. She left a couple of lamps on downstairs, then went upstairs and did the same.

Colleen came out of the bathroom wearing a red plaid nightgown and green satin slippers. "What do you think of my new pajamas?" she smirked.

Katherine burst out laughing. "You look like a Scottish elf. You didn't cut yourself on the glass, did you?"

"No. I found a plastic bag in the bathroom closet and put the glass in it. I locked it up in the closet. Don't let me forget to get rid of it in the morning. I don't want the cats to get in it."

"Cats," Katherine said darting to her room. "They've been unusually quiet." She opened the door to discover three cats curled up together on the bed, cuddled into one breathing fur ball. When she called out good night to Colleen, they didn't even flinch. "Poor kids," Katherine said. "Sleep, my darlings."

She hurriedly got ready for bed. Before slipping under the covers, she placed the alarm clock in the top drawer of the nightstand. She turned off the light and immediately fell into a deep sleep.

Chapter Six

The muffled sound of the alarm clock inside the closed drawer became an integral part of Katherine's dream. She dreamed she was sleeping in her apartment in Manhattan, and the phone kept ringing. One of the cats had pressed the off switch on the answering machine, so the phone rang for what seemed to be hours. The dream ended abruptly when Iris jumped on Katherine's chest and growled.

"Okay. Okay," Katherine said, gently pushing the Siamese off. Iris jumped on the nightstand and growled again.

Katherine got up, opened the drawer, and turned off the alarm.

"Good morning, Iris."

Iris yowled.

"Where are your sisters? Lilac? Scout?" she called.

The small lump at the foot of the bed began to move forward, tunneling in search of an opening in the feather comforter. Lilac jumped to the floor, yawned, and then did a full body stretch. "Me-yowl," she said, darting for the open door.

"Scout?" Katherine asked, worried. Iris bounded after Lilac. They thundered down the stairs.

Scout must have opened the door, Katherine thought. *Scout is running amok in a house that hasn't been cat-proofed.* She fumbled for her bathrobe and put it on. "Scout," she called from the top of the stairs.

"She's down here," Colleen said.

"Where?" Katherine said, hurrying down the stairs.

"Ah-Choo," Colleen sneezed, and then added, "We're in the kitchen having a spot of tea."

Katherine joined Colleen in the kitchen. "Cats don't drink tea," she kidded.

"Here. I'll pour you some."

"Thanks. I still don't see her."

"Waugh," Scout said, entering the room.

"Magic cat," Katherine said.

"Why did you call her that?" Colleen said, setting two cups and saucers on the table.

"Because she's already figured out how to open the door."

"What door?"

"My bedroom door."

Colleen looked guilty and said, "When I got up this morning, Scout was throwing herself against it. I thought she'd hurt herself so I let her out. She's been prowling about the place ever since."

"I kind of wanted to keep them locked up the first day in their new environment."

"Why?" Colleen asked, biting into a muffin, scattering seeds on the table.

"Because this trip has been very stressful for them. I wanted to keep them in one room of the new house for at least a day, then introduce them to the rest of the house." Katherine cleared her throat dramatically and finished, "Gradually."

Lilac chased Iris through the room. They spun their imaginary tires on the ceramic floor, caromed off the doorframe, and ran into the other room. Scout chased after them.

"My philosophy is to go for it," Colleen laughed.

Katherine studied Colleen for a moment and then said, "In the course of five minutes I've watched you devour two muffins. Are you famished?"

"They're fantastic. I've got to have this recipe."

"Mark said Patricia Marston brought them over. They're called poppy seed muffins."

"Let me get you one."

Katherine pulled up a chair and sat down. "You're all dressed—hair, make-up. What time did you get up?"

"It was early. I think six or so," Colleen said, pouring the tea. She handed Katherine a muffin.

She took a big bite, "Wow. These are good."

Colleen burst out laughing.

"What's so funny?" Katherine asked, spilling a large piece of muffin down her robe.

"You've got black seeds stuck in your teeth."

"Wonderful. I'll be flashing a big toothy smile to Mark with seeds in my teeth. No thank you," she said, pushing the muffin aside.

"There's nothing in the refrigerator except some slices of ham and cheese. We've got to get some food."

"Mark is picking me up at eleven and taking me to pick up Abigail. We can do some serious shopping when I get back."

"Give me the keys to the car. I'll pick up the groceries." Colleen hurried the last word, then sneezed.

"Are you catching a cold?"

"No, it's the dust in this place. I don't know who has been tidying up since the housekeeper has taken ill, but whoever it is, someone needs to explain to them that the vacuum cleaner works much better when it's plugged in."

"I've noticed this house needs a thorough cleaning," said Katherine.

"So, while you're off with Mr. Dreamboat, I'll forage for food and tidy up a bit."

"There's a grocery store a couple of blocks down the street. I'll pitch in as soon as I get back. What do you think of Mark?"

"That's for me to know and you to find out," Colleen said evasively. "He seems attracted to you."

"Think so?" Katherine prodded. "Actually, he's just doing his job. I'm sure he receives fees for managing my great aunt's estate."

"Me-yowl," Lilac said, trotting back into the kitchen.

"Who won the steeplechase?" Katherine asked the frisky cat. Lilac leaped up onto the counter and climbed into the kitchen sink. She began to lick the faucet.

"Yuk," Colleen grimaced.

"She used to do that at the apartment because there was a constant drip."

"Since there isn't a drip here, allow me to find this little one an alternative." Colleen got up and found a bowl in the cabinet. She filled it with water. Lilac lapped happily.

"Mum would have a fit if she knew I was setting out fine china for a cat," Colleen observed.

Katherine picked up her saucer and looked at the bottom. "I'm impressed. Haviland," she said.

"Want to see something interesting?" Colleen asked, opening several overhead cabinet doors. "Haviland china, Tiffany crystal, and a brand-new toaster and blender, still in their original boxes. To me it looks like someone came in and removed all the old stuff and replaced it with new stuff."

"That's okay with me," Katherine said. "Maybe Mrs. Marston was trying to make an impression by putting the old stuff away."

Colleen shrugged. Scout emitted a loud "waugh" from the other room.

"What are you doing in there?" Katherine called out, getting up and carrying her cup to the next room. Colleen, working on her third muffin, followed her into the room. Scout was busy watching Iris, who had jumped onto an oak roll-top desk and was struggling to keep her balance.

"There's a lot of space in this room," Colleen observed. "I think Iris is trying to tell you to use this as your office desk. I think it could be rigged to hold your computer."

"Yeah, you're right," Katherine said, running her hand over the oak desk. "Plus, I think there'd be enough room to put my printer."

"If not, there's furniture elsewhere in the house you could move in here. You can do that. I mean it's your furniture, right?" Colleen asked.

"Not yet. Remember the big terms of the will —one year. When I see Mark, I'll ask him if it's okay to move the furniture."

"But this room is virtually empty. I think you can do whatever you like in here. If you're going to live here for a year, I suggest you *live* here for a year," she stressed. "Who cares how you rearrange the furniture?"

"Exactly," Katherine agreed. "What I like about this room is that there are two doors that can be closed off from the rest of the house. If the cats are driving me crazy, I can lock them out. Oh, and that door," she said, pointing, "leads to a second-story sun porch. The cats will love it."

"Wait a minute. There're four doors in here. Where does this one go?" Colleen asked. She tried to open the door. "It's locked."

"That goes to the creepy basement. I insisted that Mark hire a locksmith to put a bolt lock on it."

"Why?"

"An ounce of prevention keeps the criminals at bay."

Colleen giggled. Somewhere in the house, a telephone rang. Scout and Lilac scampered out of the room.

"Katz, the phone. Where is it?"

"I think it's in the atrium."

"What's an atrium?"

"It's a room off the front entrance."

They left the site of Katherine's future office and headed to the atrium. The phone rang several times before Katherine answered. Iris was sitting next to it, growling.

"Thanks, Iris," she said, then into the phone, "Hello?"

"Good morning," Mark said. "I wanted to call to see how you enjoyed the first night in your new house."

"It was fine, but I can see I need to do a lot of cat-proofing."

"Or Colleen-proofing," Marked kidded. "Any more broken lamps?" he laughed.

"At least my cats haven't broken anything."

"You've just jinxed it," Colleen said in the background.

"Accidents will happen," he commented. "I just got a message from Dr. Sonny. He won't be able to release Abigail until this afternoon. I was wondering if you want to get rid of the paperwork first, get your authorization added to the house expense account, then cruise back to the house to pick up Colleen, so the two of you can join me for lunch?"

"Hold on a second," Katherine said, covering the phone. She whispered to Colleen, who was now standing nearby. "Mark has invited us to lunch."

Colleen shook her head. "I'll fix my own lunch. You two go," she said.

"Yes, of course, I'd be very pleased to join you for lunch," Katherine said, "but my friend has other plans."

"I have another call coming in. I'll see you at eleven," he said, hanging up.

"Well, Ms. Murphy," Katherine said to Colleen, "this is the first time I've ever known you to pass up lunch. Are you feeling okay?"

"I've really blown my diet eating all those muffins. Besides I have a craving for a baked potato cooked to perfection."

"How can you go wrong with a baked potato?"

"It must be slow-cooked in the oven for two hours at 325 degrees."

Katherine grinned. "Good to know. On that note, I'm going to get dressed."

"Don't forget the teeth," Colleen teased.

She headed for the main stairs and stopped abruptly on the bottom step. Something had crashed to the floor in the living room. "What now?" she asked, out loud.

Colleen came into the atrium holding two pieces of a broken *Lladro* Mother and Child figurine; the smaller piece appeared to be Mother's head. "It wasn't my fault this time."

"Oh, no. My mom used to collect these," exclaimed Katherine. "It looks like the *Peaceful Moment*."

"More like a headless moment. One of your creatures was racing through the room and knocked it off the shelf."

Lilac belted out an ear shattering me-yowl and bolted up the stairs, four steps at a time.

"I have to catch her to make sure she doesn't have any glass in her paws."

"Cats," Colleen said ruefully, shaking her head. "And you're getting another one."

* * * *

It proved to be a long, tiring day. Mark picked Katherine up promptly and drove her to his office, in one of the Victorian storefronts on Main Street. She admired his antique furniture, particularly the oak Wooten desk, with its many cubbyholes, slots and drawers. She joked that he needed a computer program to keep track of its contents in light of its complicated design. After she signed several receipt forms, Mark handed her an estate check for thirty thousand. She endorsed it and asked if he wouldn't mind taking her to the bank to set up an account. He joked that although the town had only two traffic lights, it did, however, have more than one bank. He suggested the bank where Katherine's great aunt had done business for many years.

Katherine was impressed with the friendliness of the town, but felt a little uncomfortable with strangers who either said hello to her on the street, or scrutinized her as if she were from another planet. She confessed to Mark that she could handle the greetings, but the staring routine was giving her a headache. He teased her about being a New Yorker, and she teased him about being a Hoosier. They had a quick lunch at the Red House restaurant on the edge of town, then picked up Abigail the Abyssinian.

The veterinarian's staff had made a colorful banner that said 'Abby Goes Home!' and strung it up in the front waiting room. When Dr. Sonny brought Abby out and placed her in Katherine's arms, the feline chirped in recognition, which sent Katherine into a cat cooing session lasting a full five minutes. Valerie, the receptionist, had put a green satin ribbon around Abby's neck, which complimented the ruddy-ticked color of her fur. Dr. Sonny said good-bye to his feline guest of almost two months, and Valerie gave one last pet to the purring Abyssinian.

Katherine placed Abby in the cardboard cat carrier the veterinarian clinic supplied. She was surprised Abby didn't resist, and remarked that the Siamese would have not gone in so willingly. Dr. Sonny suggested that Abigail knew she was going home. Mark, who had stood by quietly, said he thought so, too.

On the way back to the mansion, Mark suggested a late dinner at the Italian restaurant in the city, but Katherine declined. She explained she wanted to spend quality time with Abby, as well as Colleen, who would be going back to New York the following Saturday. When he dropped her off at the side door, he offered to carry Abigail inside, but Katherine said she was able. He said that if she needed anything, she should not hesitate to call. Katherine smiled and thanked him. Mark put the Honda in reverse and backed out the drive.

Katherine climbed the steps to the covered carport door and stood on the top stair, fumbling for the right key. Abigail began chirping, so Katherine gave up the search and clanged the ancient doorbell instead. Colleen opened the door, wearing a summertime barbecue apron over a green turtleneck sweater and a pair of tartan slacks.

Katherine stifled a laugh. "Where did you get that hideous looking apron?"

"I bought it at Alex's all-purpose hardware store— three bucks. Don't you think I'll set a new Erie fashion statement?"

Katherine set the cat carrier on top of the dining room table. "Something smells delicious."

"Try this on for size—tonight I'll be serving roast beef, steamed carrots, topped with an official, properly baked, potato. Is this the new fur ball?" she said, wiping her hands on her new apron. She peered into the cardboard cat carrier. "For the love of Mary, she's got bangs."

"Bangs?"

"On top of her head. They're spiked. Look," Colleen said, pointing.

"Those are stripes, not spikes," Katherine corrected. "Isn't she beautiful?"

Abigail chirped.

"Did you hear that?" Colleen asked.

"That's how she meows. Where are my other creatures?" she said, looking around.

"They were sleeping on your bed, so I simply closed the door. I figured you would want to introduce them to Ms. Bangs gradually," she said, tongue-in-cheek.

"Probably a good idea." Katherine opened the carrier door and expected Abigail to leap out, but was surprised when the cat remained inside.

"Come on, Abby. This is your home, remember?"

The Abyssinian squeezed her almond-shaped eyes, but would not budge.

"Please come out," she coaxed.

"Come out, darling," Colleen said, imitating Katherine.

Slowly Abigail sauntered out, eyeing Colleen suspiciously. She sprang off the table, darted into the living room, and began rubbing her neck on the furniture.

"I need to tend to my roast. Come in and I'll make some tea," Colleen declared as she walked back into the kitchen.

"I'll be right there." Katherine followed Abigail into the living room. "Are you happy to be home?"

Abigail came over and bumped against Katherine's legs. "Chirp," she trilled.

Katherine picked up the cat and cradled it in her arms, pulling and rubbing the fur on the back of her neck. Abby purred and squeezed her gold eyes. Then suddenly, with the full force of her back legs, she catapulted off Katherine and bounded up the stairs in a blur of ruddy brown. On the top landing of the stairwell, she belted out a loud sharp squeak, and then thundered down the hall. Katherine shrugged. *A fourth cat for the steeplechase*, she thought.

She joined Colleen in the kitchen and noticed several grocery bags on the floor. "I really appreciate your getting the groceries. Did I give you enough money?"

"Yes, with change to spare. I'm not sure people speak English around here."

150

"Why?"

"I had a hard time communicating at the grocery store. When I asked a clerk where the soda was, he directed me to the baking soda aisle. When I explained I wanted a soda—a diet soda—he said they didn't sell pop, but there were several machines up the block that did. I explained that a pop in New York was candy on a stick, and he said in Indiana that was a sucker. Did you know that in this state, bags are called sacks?"

"That's incredible," Katherine agreed. "Hey look, the kettle is boiling."

"Not until it sings," Colleen said.

"Sings?"

"It has to be boiling properly."

"For proper tea," Katherine teased.

Abigail ran through the kitchen carrying a yarn-covered ball with a bell on it. She dropped it at Katherine's feet.

"Thank you," she said, reaching down and petting the cat. Abigail bounded out of the room and shortly returned with a catnip-stuffed mouse. She jumped up onto the table, dropped it, then leaped off, racing into the dining room.

"What's with that cat?" Colleen asked.

"She's showing me her toys. She must have a secret stash somewhere like Iris had in Manhattan," Katherine said, then added, "I think I'll skip the tea. I'm really tired all of a sudden."

"Not me," Colleen said. "I've been so incredibly rejuvenated today. I think I'll get my coat on and take a walk. Care to join me?"

"It's freezing outside," Katherine warned.

"After a bit of tea," she pronounced, "a nice brisk walk will do us just fine."

"I think I'll briskly walk upstairs and join the Siamese for a little catnap."

"In their case, I think it's more like a siesta. They've been catnapping for hours."

Katherine chuckled. "Can you keep an eye on Abby?"

"Sure. I'll call you when dinner is ready."

"Wonderful," Katherine said, leaving the kitchen. She almost stumbled over Abigail, who was now playing with a tiny caged ball with a bell in it. Abby gave the toy a hard whack, which sent the ball and bell clanging underneath the Eastlake sideboard. Abby chirped and dashed into the living room. Katherine followed her. Abigail trotted over to the turret window and found a shaft of sunlight falling through it. She settled on her haunches, stretched her head and neck to the sunlight, and closed her eyes.

"I'll leave you here to bask," Katherine said.

"Chirp," Abby said softly, without opening her eyes.

Katherine studied Abby for a moment and thought about how attached she was to her already. Walking upstairs, she quietly opened the bedroom door and found three Siamese sleeping in a huddle on the tall bed. Katherine crawled on top of the bed and curled up beside them. She fell asleep immediately. She slept for several hours when Colleen shouted from the foot of the stairs.

"Dinner is served," she said dramatically. "Katz and all kitty cats proceed to the kitchen."

"Okay," Katherine said sleepily. Opening her eyes, she discovered a fourth feline party in her bed—a ruddy, gold-eyed beauty, sleeping idyllically, paw-to-paw with Lilac.

"What a lovely twosome," she admired.

Iris stormed out from under the covers, observed the interloper, and hissed ferociously. Abigail held her ground while Lilac quivered and began to whine.

"Iris, be nice," Katherine warned.

"Asp," Abigail said menacingly.

Katherine said to Abigail, "That's Iris, not Isis," and then to Iris, "Iris, this is Abby. Abby is the princess of the Nile, and you my snarling beauty are the princess of Siam."

"Hiss," Iris replied loudly.

"Asp." Abigail now sounded merely suspicious.

Iris leaped off of the bed and took a position on the floor, where she could watch the newcomer's every move.

Scout, who was sleeping on Katherine's side, opened one eye, emitted a "waugh," then went back to sleep. Abigail licked the frightened Lilac on the head. Katherine moved them next to Scout and they continued their bathing session. She got out of bed and made her way downstairs.

Colleen and Katherine relaxed over dinner and spent the rest of the evening in the parlor, sipping hot chocolate in front of the fireplace. Their quiet time was interrupted several times by cat spats in other rooms, mostly between Iris and Abigail. The throaty rumble of Iris's growls and snarls, and the counter-defensive chirping of Abigail became progressively less frequent, as even the pugnacious Iris seemed to bore of the confrontations. Abigail held her own and was not the least bit intimidated by the loud bluffs of the seal-point Siamese.

It was late when Katherine and Colleen went to bed. Before going to their rooms, they vowed to sleep in late the next morning.

"Good night, Katz," Colleen said, walking down the hall.

"Waugh," Scout said, following her.

Colleen went into her room, but before she could shut her door, she had to evict the unwanted guest. "Sorry, this room is a no-cat zone," Colleen said, escorting Scout out and shutting the door.

"Come on, kids. Let's get our pajamas on. That includes you, Scout." Katherine called from the end of the hall.

"Waugh," Scout protested. She trotted down the hall. Lilac and Abigail were already in the bedroom and were crunching on dry food from their dishes while Iris peered down from the edge of the Eastlake dresser—her head angled downward like a vulture's—ready to pounce on the unsuspecting orphan below.

"Iris," Katherine warned. "Be good. Remember, Abby is from Egypt and she might send you another snake."

"Yowl," Iris complained.

* * * *

The next morning Katherine struggled out of bed at ten-thirty. She met Colleen in the hallway. Colleen's face was smeared with a green facial mask.

"You look a fright," Katherine said. "I hate to tell you this, but someone really screwed up at the cosmetic counter."

"It's natural clay," Colleen boasted.

"Clay is gray or red. Trust me, you're *green.*"

Scout trotted down the hall and stopped dead in her tracks. She gazed intently at Colleen, then spat a hiss. She scurried downstairs.

"I have to wash this mess off."

"Did I hear the phone ring?" Katherine asked.

"You won't believe who called me."

"Who has the number here?"

"My Mum gave it to Jacky, who gave it to Mario. He called me. Can you believe it? He asked me out for next weekend."

"For a second date? Good work, Mario."

"You won't believe what he sang to me?"

"Let me guess—a bit of *Gangnam Style*?"

"*Uptown Girl.* She's been living in her uptown world . . ." Colleen launched into a female rendition of Billy Joel's famous song, complete with Irish brogue intonations.

"Stop," Katherine said, covering her ears.

Colleen exploded with laughter and went into the bathroom.

* * * *

For a couple of hours during the afternoon, the outside temperature warmed up to forty degrees, which allowed Katherine to open the front door for half an hour to air out the stuffy house. While Katherine was busy cleaning upstairs, Colleen was working downstairs. They had flipped a coin—heads for upstairs and tails for downstairs. Katherine picked heads and was relieved she didn't have to tackle the kitchen. Colleen was elated that she didn't have to do cat litter patrol. Every once in a while, the two would stop to take a few sips of sweet tea, call up and down to each other, and discuss the latest antics by one or more of the four cats. Each discussion began with "You'll not believe what so-and-so just did." They would laugh and then resume their frenzied cleaning activity.

Occasionally the Siamese would hinder their efforts. Lilac was terrified of the vacuum cleaner and had to be consoled after each room was swept. In the kitchen while Colleen tried to sweep, Iris stalked the broom. Several times she pounced on the bristles, used them as a springboard, and scurried to another part of the house. Scout prowled restlessly, walking back and forth the full length of the living room. She stopped to rub each piece of furniture with her jaw, marking and remarking her new territory. Each time a piece of furniture was waxed, Scout would dance across it, leaving fresh paw prints in her wake. Meanwhile, Abigail had climbed to the top of a window valance and quietly observed the scene below.

After several hours, Katherine called from the top of the stairs, "Are you finished with the vacuum cleaner?"

"Yes, Katz," Colleen yelled from the walk-in closet in the atrium. "Come down here for a minute. I want you to show you something."

Katherine hurried down the stairs two at a time, "What?"

Colleen pointed at a new Hoover packing box. "I had to unpack it to use it."

"Wow, no wonder the house was so dusty," Katherine joked. "Mark mentioned that my great aunt made a charitable gift to some organization, which would explain all the empty closets and replacement appliances."

"Can't complain about new," Colleen shrugged with a smile.

At two p.m., Colleen and Katherine stopped long enough to eat sandwiches and then returned to their work. At four they threw in the towel. Colleen went off to the kitchen to brew some flavored coffee, while Katherine put away the vacuum sweeper in the near empty cloak closet. When she joined Colleen in the kitchen she inhaled deeply. "Hazelnut. My favorite."

In another room, something heavy crashed to the floor.

"Did you hear that?" Katherine asked.

"What have they done now?" Colleen threw her hands in the air. "Shouldn't we go upstairs and check?"

"No, it sounded more like it came from the basement."

"It's probably just an icicle falling off the gutter. I saw some really big ones out there," Colleen said.

There was another loud thump.

"*That* didn't sound like an icicle," Katherine said, bolting out of the room. She ran up the stairs and went directly to the bedroom. The Siamese were curled up and sleeping on the bed. She then went back downstairs.

"What did they break this time?" Colleen asked.

"Nothing. They're asleep. It must have been something out on the street. Have you seen Abby?"

"She's not with the Siamese?"

"No, she's not."

"Last time I saw her, she was prowling around like Scout does, going from room to room, sniffing everything."

"Abby," Katherine called, concerned.

There was a loud thud nearby.

"That didn't come from the basement," Colleen said.

"It sounded like it came from the living room, but I distinctly shut all of those pocket doors."

They rushed into the atrium, slid open one of the pocket doors, and then darted inside to find Abigail sitting demurely in a large flowerpot that contained a tall rubber plant. The surrounding planters had been turned over— their soil spread everywhere. The remnants of shredded plants were strewn across the oriental carpet.

"What a mess," Katherine said, aghast.

"Chirp," Abigail announced proudly from the flowerpot.

"'Tis the worse mess I've ever seen," Colleen noted. "How did she get in here?"

"I must have closed her in when I shut the doors."

"Abby," Katherine scolded, walking over to the guilty-looking cat. Abigail leapt out of the flowerpot and rocketed out of the room.

"I hate to tell you this, Katz, but I think this mess requires more than the Hoover. We need the help of your handy dandy man."

"I have his business card. I'll give him a call," Katherine said wearily. She went to the atrium phone and dialed Cokey Cokenberger's number. A male voice answered on the third ring.

"Cokenberger Contracting," he said.

"Hello, Mr. Cokenberger. This is Katherine Kendall."

"I'm sorry, I'm the son. Let me get my Dad." He put the phone down, then yelled, "Dad, you're wanted on the phone. It's that lady from the pink house."

"Just a second, Tommy," Cokey called to his son. "And it's 'Ms. Kendall,' not *that lady*," he corrected.

The son got back on the line. "He's in the kitchen. Ah, here he is," he said handing his father the phone.

"Hello, Ms. Kendall?" he said in an out-of-breath but friendly voice.

"Hello, Mr. Cokenberger."

"Cokey. Call me Cokey," he insisted.

"I'm sorry to disturb you at home, but I have a bit of problem over here at the house. One of my cats decided to rearrange the flowerpots in the living room. I need your help to carry what remains of the potted plants to a place where the cats can't get them."

"What happened?" he asked, mystified.

"Abigail dumped all of the flower pots and has made an incredible mess. There's potting soil everywhere."

"That sweet little girl? Surely not," he chuckled. "I'm just finishing my supper and I'll be over directly. I'll bring my Shop-Vac." He hung up.

"Supper," Katherine said. "It's not even five," she said looking at her watch.

"Katz, look," Colleen said, pulling a newspaper clipping out of one of the unearthed flower pots.

"What is it?"

"It's an engagement notice. I can hardly read it." She took it over to one of the windows. "Vivian Marston announces the March wedding of her daughter Patricia to James Edward Cokenberger."

"Handy Dandy! Our Cokey?" Katherine said. "Shhh, I just heard someone pull in. I think he's here."

"Already," Colleen confirmed.

The doorbell clanged noisily. Katherine rushed to the side door and unlocked it. "I'm so glad you could make it," she said.

"Show me the disaster site," he said merrily.

Katherine escorted him into the living room.

"Looks like a tornado hit," he exclaimed.

"Look what I found in one of the pots," Colleen said, holding up the aged article. "It's an announcement with your name on it. Strange place for a newspaper clipping, don't ya think?"

Cokey became quiet. He squinted to read the article, "I'm sorry, I left my reading glasses at home."

"It's your engagement notice to your wife," Colleen blurted. "Do you want this clipping?"

"My 'wife' and I were never engaged," he coughed nervously. "I think you've found one of my skeletons in the closet," he said solemnly. "I was engaged to Patricia Marston for a brief time. We broke up years ago, and I married my only wife, Margaret."

"Oh, I see," Colleen said, embarrassed.

Cokey looked at the floor.

"You'll have to bring Margaret over so we can meet her," Katherine said, breaking the uncomfortable silence.

"My wife would love to meet you, as well as my kids. They're nuts about cats."

"Now I've put my foot in it," Colleen said. "I'm terribly sorry."

"We didn't realize," Katherine said apologetically.

"I'm surprised a newspaper clipping would survive being buried in a flowerpot since the Stone Age," he laughed, then added, "I have to go to my truck. I'll be right back."

Once Cokey had left the room, Katherine said, "Great, Colleen. He's probably never coming back."

"I didn't know it," Colleen said innocently.

163

"Shhh, here he comes."

Cokey returned, carrying a large Shop-Vac. "You ladies might want to leave the room," he advised. "This is very loud." He plugged in the Shop-Vac and began to carefully vacuum the soil from the oriental carpet.

Colleen went back into the parlor while Katherine began searching each room for Abigail. "Abby," she called over the deafening drone of the Shop-Vac. She searched the kitchen—no Abby. She circled the house, going from room to room, calling the cat's name—no response. She walked upstairs and was surprised to see Abby sitting outside her bedroom door.

"The Siamese are in there," Katherine said. "Do you want to take a nap with them?" She stroked the silky fur of the Abyssinian.

"Chirp," Abigail said in agitation. She stood up on her hind legs and reached for the door handle.

Katherine opened the door and Abigail bounded inside. The three Siamese woke up, but Lilac and Scout immediately went back to sleep. Iris hissed and then yawned. She put one paw over her eye and curled up closer to Scout, then went back to sleep. Abigail jumped up on the bed and walked a few feet from the sleeping cats. She began purring, tucked her paws underneath her, and closed her eyes.

"Sweet dreams, my darlings," Katherine said. She shut the four cats in the bedroom and went back down to the atrium. "I can't understand why she did that."

"What, I can't hear you?" Colleen said struggling to hear.

"Why did Abigail destroy the plants?" Katherine shouted.

Colleen shrugged.

Cokey Cokenberger turned off the noisy vacuum and entered the room. "I'm bankin' that the only plant that will survive is that big old rubber plant. I'll take it down to the solarium."

"Solarium? Where's that?" Katherine asked, perplexed.

"It's that room with the metal door to the outside; the one with all the windows. Mrs. Colfax called it the solarium."

"Thanks, but I really didn't like the idea of plants being up here anyway. I've found that cats and plants don't mix."

"I'll roll this rug up and take it home. I can have the carpet cleaning service pick it up. I'll bring it back good as new."

"Yes, please," Katherine said.

After Cokey left the room, Colleen whispered behind him, "I wonder why they broke up? Inquiring minds want to know."

"You mean incredibly nosy minds," Katherine countered. "Is there a date on the clipping?"

"No, the date is torn off. Why do you think it was buried in the flowerpot?"

"'Tis a mystery."

Cokey slipped into the room holding a dirty stuffed bear. "I found this in one of the broken flowerpots," he said.

Katherine and Colleen exchanged curious glances.

"I just saw that hanging in the bathroom," Colleen said.

"Oh, no—not Lilac's bear," Katherine said, taking the stuffed toy. "This is one of my cat's favorite toys," she explained. "I've already given it one bath today when Lilac dropped in the dirty mop water. Now I'll have to give it another one."

Cokey laughed and left the room.

"Did you notice," Colleen began whispering, "that when he came into the room, we didn't hear him?"

"I noticed that. I don't know how he does it. Every time I take a step, the floorboards squeak bloody murder.

Maybe we should check to see if he leaves a reflection in the mirror," Katherine kidded.

"I vote we move these Queen Anne wing chairs so we can see whoever comes into the room. I don't like having my back to a door."

"Spoken like a true New Yorker."

Katherine easily moved one of the chairs. Colleen moved the other chair a few inches but stopped when she heard something drop to the floor. She reached down and picked up an old-fashioned, flip-top cigarette lighter.

"Did that come from inside the chair?" Katherine asked.

"Here, help me tip it over," Colleen said. After the two of them flipped the chair onto its side, they discovered a tear in the lining.

"Did one of the cats do this?" Colleen asked suspiciously.

"I can't tell if it's a cat tear or an old age tear," Katherine said.

"There's something hanging down from it." Colleen pulled out a plastic object.

"My night retainer!" Katherine exclaimed.

"Oh, that's disgusting. Take it," Colleen said scrunching up her face.

"I'll bet you five bucks Iris stole it out of my bag and stashed it in this chair."

"She doesn't waste any time hiding her loot," Colleen observed. She continued feeling around and pulled out a caged ball with a bell inside. "Wasn't the cat with bangs playing with this earlier? Care to pay me in singles or a crisp Lincoln back?"

"Abigail, too," Katherine gasped. "Now I have two kleptomaniacs."

"Who do you think this lighter belongs to?"

"It looks like 14-karat gold plating. It probably belonged to one of my great aunt's guests. Mark said she entertained frequently."

"No, wait. There's an inscription—*To Cokey with Love.* There's a letter after that but it's been scratched out," Colleen said as she handed the lighter to Katherine.

"Listen, I'll try and catch him before he leaves," Katherine said, heading for the door.

"I guess you'll have to do that tomorrow."

"Why?"

"He just backed out of the driveway," Colleen said, pulling the lace panel aside and looking out the window.

"I'd better check to see if he locked the exterior door to the basement on his way out."

"Wait. I'll go too, but first let me get my EMF meter," Colleen said cheerfully. She bolted out of the room and rushed up the stairs.

Katherine called after her. "Seriously, do you think a ghost would prefer the basement over being up here?" She laughed.

"I'm coming, I'm coming. Don't go down there without me," Colleen yelled from upstairs.

"Okay, whatever. But, if you get any ghost readings, I'm throwing that thing out into the snow," Katherine teased.

Chapter Seven

By Wednesday, Katherine and Colleen were bored out of their minds. The ghost-hunting adventure to the basement had been a bust. Colleen complained that she wasn't getting a reading anywhere in the house. Even the dusty attic didn't set off the EMF meter.

Katherine's laptop was useless because the cable company hadn't connected its service. No email. No high-speed Internet. Katherine's thumbs were cramping from texting friends; Colleen was tired of playing the same apps on her phone.

The boxes from New York hadn't arrived, so there was nothing to unpack and put away. The house was sparkling clean; the rugs swept, the floors mopped.

The boredom had even spread to the cats, who didn't want to get off Katherine's bed to eat their breakfast. Colleen suggested some retail therapy, so the two got into the Toyota and drove to the city. Katherine needed to visit the home improvement store, and Colleen wanted to shop for clothes. By noon, they were famished and stopped at a chain Italian restaurant. Colleen talked about her crush on Mario, and Katherine talked about Mark Dunn. She wasn't sure about him just yet, but she admitted she was kind of interested.

Just before dark, they drove back to Erie. It took a while to unload the car, which was stuffed with their new purchases. Afterward, they decided to go see a movie. The town of Erie boasted one of the finest theaters in the state. It was built in the Art Deco period and had been painstakingly restored by its current owners. The movie was a romantic suspense thriller with Colleen's favorite Irish actor. Katherine munched on Twizzlers, and Colleen ate an entire bucket of buttered popcorn. Later she complained that she had totally blown her diet. They were in a happy mood when they pulled into the driveway of the pink mansion.

"Didn't we leave some lights on?" Katherine asked, suddenly worried.

"Yes," Colleen said uneasily.

"It's pitch-dark inside. Do you think there's been a power failure?"

"No, not really," Colleen said, looking around. "The neighbors' lights are on."

"This gives me the creeps. Something is not right here."

They quickly got out of the Toyota and paused on the bottom landing of the covered carport steps. Katherine rummaged in her bag and found her keys. "Dammit, it's so dark. I can't find the right one."

"Don't even bother," Colleen said. "The door's open."

"Oh, no! Do you think somebody broke into the house?"

"Call the cops," Colleen said, starting to jog down the driveway. "I can't because my cell is upstairs on the charger."

Katherine punched in 911.

The 911 operator answered, "What's your emergency?"

"I'm calling from 512 Lincoln Street. Someone has broken into my house."

"Stay where you are and I'll send someone."

"Okay, thanks," Katherine said, and then called to her friend, who was hovering at the end of the drive. "Come back, Colleen. The police will be here in a minute."

As the two waited, an Erie police cruiser pulled into the driveway. When the patrolman got out, they rushed over to him. A second officer got out of the car and put his baton through a loop on his parka.

"I'm Chief Charles London and this is Officer Dan Glover. I normally don't answer these kinds of calls but tonight it's my turn to ride shotgun. We're kind of short-handed here in Erie. Which one of you made the call?"

"I did," Katherine said. "My name is Katherine Kendall. This is my friend Colleen Murphy. My late great aunt left me this house."

"Yes, I heard about that. What seems to be the problem here?"

"We came home and found all the lights were out. And the side door was open."

"Big old house like this, I'd say you probably tripped a breaker. Did you possibly forget to shut the door?" he asked.

"I distinctly remember locking it," she answered.

"Well, now, ladies, we'll go in and have a look. You stay out here."

Chief London and Officer Glover entered the house. Katherine and Colleen remained in the driveway, watching lights being turned on throughout the house.

"So much for the 'breaker' theory," Colleen observed.

"What if something happened to my cats?" Katherine worried.

"When we left, to go see the movie, you put them in the bedroom. I shut the door," Colleen reminded.

"If a criminal got in, Scout and Lilac would hide under the bed. Iris would challenge him and possibly do battle. But, Abby, she's so incredibly friendly, she'd probably lick his hand," Katherine said apprehensively.

Officer Glover returned. "You two want to come in?"

"Yes, it's freezing out here," Colleen complained.

The chief stood in the dining room, tugging at his short beard. "Well, it wasn't a power outage. We checked out two floors; didn't find anything suspicious. Does anyone else have keys to this house?"

"Not anymore," Katherine said. "The locks have been changed."

"Well, everything seems okay now. If you find anything missing, feel free to give us a call."

"Thank you," Katherine said.

"Lock up behind us," he said. He tipped his hat and left.

Officer Glover said good-bye and Katherine bolted the door.

"That's a standard phrase in this town," she noted. "Mark said it, too."

"What, 'good-bye?'" Colleen asked.

"No, lock the door behind me."

"Waugh," Scout cried meekly from the top of the atrium curio cabinet. She was sitting like an Egyptian statue next to the telephone. Iris jumped up beside her. Katherine noticed that Iris's tail was three times its normal size. Abby and Lilac entered, trotting side-by-side. They looked like two horses of a different kind. "Me-yowl," Lilac said to Abby's "Chirp."

Walking over to Scout, Katherine asked, "How did you guys get out of your room?" As Katherine reached over to pick up Scout, the lights went off. "I don't freaking believe this," she said.

Colleen panicked and stumbled over a chair. Lilac and Abigail catapulted off the dining room wall and rocketed up the stairs. Iris or Scout misjudged the bottom step and caromed off the Turkish nook table, knocking it over in her wake. Katherine heard more feline feet thundering up the stairs.

"Colleen, are you okay?"

"I'm good, but what just happened?"

"It's probably electrical," Katherine reassured. "We have to go down in the basement and find the circuit breaker box."

"No way," Colleen said. "How are we going to see? It's totally dark."

"Okay, let me think. I remember seeing a small flashlight hanging on the atrium door. Just stay here a minute and I'll try to find it," Katherine said bravely, feeling her way into the atrium. When she found the flashlight, she turned it on and began flashing the beam back and forth in the room. When she joined Colleen, something loud crashed in the basement.

"Oh, the saints preserve us. We'll all be killed!" Colleen screamed, running from the house.

Katherine ran after her, slamming the door. "Colleen! Stop!"

"Are you crazy? We need to get those officers back here."

"We can't keep calling the cops every time we hear a little bit of noise or have a power failure. The officers turned on all the lights. It was probably too much for the system."

"So?" Colleen said, terrified.

"So, like the chief said, it's an old house. A power surge most likely tripped the circuit breaker. We've got to go down in the basement and check it out."

"I can't believe we're going to go root around in that dark basement with just a flashlight," Colleen complained. "It's creepy enough in the daylight."

"Which would you rather do, go with me, or stand out here and freeze to death?" Katherine countered.

Colleen mounted the covered carport steps, but Katherine kept walking down the driveway. "Where are you going?" she asked.

"Remember? There's a door in the back of the house. You can get to the basement from there."

Walking to the rear of the house, they found the door and unlocked it. Stepping in, Colleen held the flashlight while Katherine headed to the mechanical room. Colleen swept the flashlight beam around erratically.

"Gimme that," Katherine said, taking it away from her. "This isn't a laser light show." She concentrated the beam along the walls in search of the circuit breaker box.

"What does it look like?" Colleen asked.

"It's just a gray metal box against a wall with a bunch of switches on it."

"Like that?" Colleen said, pointing to a wall near the water heater.

"Where?"

"Over there by that tank thing, and that big green plastic bag on the floor."

Katherine walked over and found the gray rectangular panel. She played the flashlight beam over each breaker switch; all of them indicated the power was on. She looked at the main switch at the top of the panel. The breaker was not tripped, but the switch was off. She pushed the switch up with a clank and the basement lights came on.

"For the love of Mary!" Colleen screamed.

"What now?" Katherine said, getting annoyed.

"There's a foot sticking out under that bag!" Colleen pointed toward the water heater.

Katherine got down on her knees and partially moved the plastic garbage bag aside. She stared mutely at a lifeless body on the concrete floor.

"Is she dead?" Colleen asked, as she took a cautious step forward.

Katherine nodded. "This is so tragic. Poor Mrs. Marston."

"Who?"

"Vivian Marston. My great aunt's housekeeper."

"I thought you said she was in the hospital."

"Last time I asked about her condition, Mark said she'd been moved to the Erie Nursing Home. He said she was in a coma."

"Coma?" Colleen asked, stunned. "Then what's she doing here?"

"I don't know," Katherine said, baffled. She fished out her cell and called 911 again. "Please send the officers back to 512 Lincoln Street. We've found a body in the basement."

They heard a police siren in the distance. Within a few minutes, the chief's cruiser pulled up and parked behind Katherine's car. She ran out and waved them to the rear door. Chief London and Officer Glover got out and hurriedly ran into the basement.

"Don't touch anything," the chief barked at Katherine and Colleen. "I used to be a detective in the city before the Mayor appointed me the new chief." He brusquely strode over to the body, pulled on a pair of blue latex gloves, and stooped down, looking closely at the face. "I know who this is," he said. "It's Vivian Marston." He looked up at Katherine and asked, "Why is she wedged next to the water heater?"

"I don't know," Katherine answered sadly.

The stillness of the room was shattered by the bloodcurdling yowl of a terrified feline upstairs. One of the cats was throwing her body against the door at the top of the basement stairs. The door led to Katherine's office.

Officer Glover unsnapped the flap on his holster and started up the stairs.

"Stop!" Katherine pleaded. "It's my cat behind the door. Please don't shoot."

"Sounded like a woman screaming," he said suspiciously.

The hysterical cry was heard again. "Waugh," Scout shrieked.

"It's Scout—my Siamese. She's very upset. I have to go and comfort her," she said, heading for the windowed sunroom.

"Where are you going?" he yelled.

"Please, Officer, the door is bolt-locked from the other side. I have to go back out of the house to the side door, go to my office and unlock the door."

"No, it's not locked," Officer Glover said as he pushed open the door. Suddenly a streak of brown shot down the basement steps like a bullet. The officer grabbed the handrail and nearly lost his balance as he sidestepped the hysterical ten-pound Siamese.

"Scout," Katherine cried anxiously.

Scout ran past her and went directly to the body. She arched her back, and with all four legs stiffened, began bouncing up and down in some kind of bizarre dance, with her eyes fixed on the corpse.

"Why is she doing that?" Colleen asked, frightened.

"Get that cat away from the crime scene," the chief shouted in exasperation.

Katherine rushed over and reached down to pick up the terror-stricken cat. Scout's V-shaped jaw was tightly clamped on a small silver key ring with a charm attached. With one hand, she began massaging Scout's mouth. Scout spit out the key ring and then bit Katherine hard on the hand. "Ouch," she cried. Scout sprang off Katherine and resumed her macabre dance. She began uttering a throaty, morbid-sounding wail.

The chief seemed angry, but reluctant to move closer to Scout. He said to Katherine, "Give me one good reason why I shouldn't call Animal Control."

"Oh, no! Please don't. She's just frightened," Katherine pleaded. "Scout, darling," she said gently. Scout gave one last Halloween lurch, then trotted back to Katherine. "Waugh," the Siamese said in her normal voice. Katherine picked her up and began stroking her. Scout was trembling. "It's okay, baby," she cooed. Scout thrust her head against Katherine's forehead, then nuzzled her head into the crook of Katherine's arm.

"Well, lookie here," the chief said, picking up the key ring. "It seems like the charm part is broken."

Officer Glover explained, "No, not really. The charm is the right side of a heart. When my wife and I were dating, we gave each other one of these. You join them together and it makes a heart shape. We had each other's initials engraved on them and wore them around our necks."

"I can't read the engraving on this one," the chief said, squinting.

"It's the letter M," Officer Glover read.

"M for Marston. Must belong to Vivian," the chief said.

"Or Vivian's daughter, Patricia," Katherine added. "She's also an employee here. Maybe she dropped it the last time she was here."

The chief ignored Katherine's remark and said, "I can't decide if this key ring was on the victim's body or if the cat picked it up elsewhere. Dan, what do you think?"

Officer Glover shrugged. "Maybe when Vivian fell, she dropped the key ring."

"Who carries around a key ring without a key; there has to be one around here somewhere," the chief said, scanning the floor. "Eureka," he said, stooping down again. He picked up a key that was previously unnoticed.

Katherine reached in her pocket and pulled out her house key. "Chief, the key you just found looks like a copy of my house key," Katherine said. "Can I compare the two?"

"Nope," he answered, dropping the key and the key ring in an evidence bag.

Colleen said tensely, "If I have to stay here a moment longer, I'm sure to faint."

"Go upstairs," the chief said. "You too," he said to Katherine. "And take that damned cat. Wait for us there."

Colleen was already at the top of the stairs. Katherine followed her, still holding the quivering Siamese.

"Wait a minute," he called after Katherine. "What did you say your name is? You told me earlier but I'd forgotten."

"Katherine Kendall," she said firmly.

"Yes, good to know," he said gruffly. "Now go on upstairs."

The chief said to Officer Glover, "We need to get a hold of the State Police. We'll need a detective to help us out with this case. Also, call the coroner," he instructed.

Katherine closed the door and whispered to Colleen, "Did you hear that? They're calling the State Police for a detective. I can't believe this," she said, stunned. "Do you think they suspect us of murder?"

Colleen was nervously pacing back and forth. "Surely not, Katz. Maybe it's standard procedure to call in somebody else. Are you sure we want to stay here tonight? Couldn't we check in to that bed and breakfast place?"

Katherine did not answer. She kissed Scout on the head and set her down. Scout bounded off into the living room. Katherine and Colleen followed her.

"Wasn't it called the Little Tomato? Couldn't we stay there tonight?" Colleen pleaded.

"You may if you like, but I'm not going to allow this to drive me out of this house," Katherine said determinedly. "I vote we stay and search the rest of the house ourselves. It's obvious the chief didn't, or else he would have found Mrs. Marston in the basement."

"You got that straight."

"First, we need to make sure the other cats are okay. Help me find them, and then we'll close them up in my bedroom."

Colleen relaxed a little and said, "Maybe we should turn off some of these lights so they don't blow up the circuit box again."

"I hate to tell you this, but someone deliberately turned off the main power switch."

Colleen's eyes widened. "No! Tell me true."

"We were *not* the only ones in the house when the power went off."

"Katz, you're scaring me."

Scout trailed Katherine as she moved from room to room, calling for the other cats. "Waugh," Scout eventually cried, growing tired of the search. She darted up the stairs.

"The cats must be upstairs already," Colleen suggested.

Katherine climbed the stairs and discovered her bedroom door closed. She momentarily stood outside. "Lilac . . . Iris . . . Abby," she called.

"Me-yowl," a muffled voice cried. "Yowl," Iris demanded from inside the room.

"This is odd," she said to Colleen, who was several feet behind her. "Why is this door closed? When we came back from the movie, the cats had gotten out of the room and were downstairs. Now, they're closed up again. What is going on?" Katherine asked, as she hesitantly turned the doorknob.

Katherine opened the door and Iris flung out. The fur on her back was bristled and she was quivering. Katherine picked her up and held her for a moment. "Colleen, can you catch the light?"

Colleen turned on the overhead chandelier. They both gasped. The room was in shambles. The nightstand was overturned and its contents strewn across the floor. The mattress was pulled half off its foundation. The closet door was open, and Katherine's clothing was ripped off their hangers, piled into a heap in the middle of the floor.

One of the Eastlake armoire's doors was open, with contents spilling out. The vandal had also tipped over the litter box and had dumped the cats' water bowl over the marble dresser; the water now dripped slowly onto the wool oriental carpet.

Iris struggled to be put down. Katherine set her down next to Scout who began to furiously groom the top of Iris's head.

"Lilac . . . Abby," Katherine called frantically. Lilac and Abigail both crawled slowly out from under the bed.

Katherine picked up Abigail and quickly checked her out. When she reached for Lilac, the Siamese darted away.

"Are they okay?"

"Yes, but I'm not," Katherine said angrily. "I'm going to get to the bottom of this."

"Why would anyone want to do this?" Colleen asked, grabbing Katherine's terry cloth bathrobe. She began soaking up water from atop the dresser.

"I don't have a clue, but maybe someone wants to scare me out of this house."

"But that doesn't make any sense." Colleen stopped sopping up water.

"I think we should leave this room, and have the chief take a look at it."

"We can put the cats in my room," Colleen proposed.

"No, that's not necessary. How about that other bedroom at the end of the hall? The one with the super tall headboard?"

"I'll carry the ladies' room," Colleen said, lifting the empty litter box. "Do we have any stuff to put in it?"

"Cat litter? There's some in the closet next to your room." Katherine put down Abigail, who quickly moved ahead to join Lilac in the hallway. They rubbed noses. Scout and Iris crept behind Colleen down the hall.

"Check your bedroom. Is everything okay?" Katherine called after her.

Colleen went into her room and shouted, "I don't believe this. Someone dumped my suitcase. My clothes are everywhere."

"What?" Katherine said, rushing down the hall. She found Colleen standing next to the bed, holding what remained of her smashed EMF meter.

"Oh, no they didn't," Colleen said furiously.

"Who would do this?"

"And it was freaking new."

"But why would someone break your ghost gizmo and not your cell phone? Look, it's still on the charger."

Colleen grabbed her phone and quickly put it in her pocket.

"We need to tell the chief right away, but first help me get the cats in their new room before something else happens."

Katherine went back to her ransacked room and picked up the empty water bowl. She juggled the bowl, cat food dishes, and the heavy plastic bottle of spring water and made her way down the hall. She nearly tripped over Scout, who had shot down the hall.

"Waugh," Scout cried.

"Are you thirsty, Scout?" Katherine asked, setting the load down on the floor next to the antique bed. She opened the spring water bottle and filled the cats' water bowl. Meanwhile, Colleen had found the litter and poured a small amount into the box.

"Put in more than that," Katherine advised.

Lilac and Abby had jumped on the unmade bed and were rolling back and forth.

"Look at those two creatures already at home on the bed as if they know they're sleeping here tonight," Colleen ventured.

"It seems very cold in this room. For starters, I'm going to need a few blankets. Later, I need to find some clean sheets to put on it."

"In the meantime, I have something warm for them to sleep on," Colleen said leaving the room. She returned carrying a cable-knit sweater.

"Not your best sweater," Katherine warned.

"It's only for a couple of hours. How can they possibly hurt it?" she insisted, making a little nest on top of the bed.

Scout jumped onto the bed and began sniffing every inch of the mattress cover. Meanwhile, Iris leapt up onto the Renaissance Revival dresser and was rubbing her jaw against one of its corners. Abigail and Lilac immediately dove for the sweater. While Abby push-pawed the new bed, Lilac positioned herself in the middle of the sweater and settled into a tight circle, lying on her side.

"I'm so thankful that whoever did this didn't hurt my cats," Katherine said worriedly.

"Katz, don't think about that now. Your cats are okay."

Fishing her cell phone out of her back pocket, Katherine said, "I'm going to call Mark." Mark's cell rang once, then went directly into voice mail. Katherine said in a nervous voice, "Please come to the house. There's been a terrible tragedy."

"Ms. Kendall," the chief shouted from downstairs. "Could you please come down?"

"Him again?" Colleen mumbled.

Iris's throat rumbled with a ferocious growl. "It's okay, baby," Katherine soothed.

They shut the cats in the room and went downstairs to the atrium.

"I need to ask you a few questions," the chief said, leaning against one of the closed pocket doors.

"Sure," Katherine said. "I need to speak to you about something, also."

The chief looked at her expectantly, as if she were about to make a confession.

"Somebody ransacked my bedroom," Katherine said. "I'm surprised you didn't notice it when you searched the house."

He hesitated for a moment and then said defensively, "There was a room upstairs on the left that I didn't check because the door was locked."

"My bedroom door was locked?" Katherine asked, surprised.

"I knocked but nobody answered."

"When I came up here, a few minutes ago, the door was closed but not locked."

The chief shrugged. "I heard a cat in there, so I figured you'd locked it in there."

Katherine and Colleen exchanged questioning looks.

Officer Glover came in. "Coroner is here. Do you wish to speak to him?"

"Yeah, in a few minutes."

Officer Glover nodded and went back down to the basement.

"Let's have a look at that bedroom," Chief London said.

Katherine directed him upstairs to her great aunt's former bedroom.

He quietly looked around, tugged his beard, and then stared into her eyes. "You're not into drugs, are you?"

Katherine's jaw dropped. She replied indignantly, "I'm most certainly not."

"Routine question when I find something like this," he explained. "Do you have any idea what they were looking for?"

"No," she said. "What would they want with my clothes? I just hung them up yesterday. The rest of my stuff isn't coming until tomorrow."

The chief nodded and said gently, "I'm sorry to be so rough on you, but we haven't had a murder in Erie for a long, long time."

"What do you mean?" Katherine asked warily.

"It's simple. Vivian Marston died in a very suspicious and apparently unnatural way in your house," he said. "Now, you tell me, what would you think if you were in my shoes?"

"I don't know why she was in my house. My attorney said she was in the nursing home."

"Yes, Vivian was," Mark Dunn said, entering the room. "Hi, Chief. Dan let me in through the basement." He turned to Katherine. "I was just a few blocks away when I got your message." Mark glanced around the vandalized room, moved over to Katherine's side, and whispered, "Love what you've done with the place."

Katherine attempted a smile.

The chief looked at Mark. "Was she or wasn't she in a nursing home?"

"Yes, but she was discovered missing from the home around seven p.m."

Colleen, who previously had been standing outside, suddenly bustled into the room and said animatedly, "'Tis nonsense, I tell you. How can a woman who is in a coma go missing from her bed?"

"Good question," the chief said.

Mark put up his hands. "Up to a few minutes ago, I was at the nursing home. I talked to everyone on the staff, and no one could figure out what happened to her. When I left the home, the nurse in charge was calling Vivian's daughter, Patricia. I suggested that they also call the police."

"What is your involvement in this?" the chief asked.

"As you know, my law firm has represented the Colfax family for a number of years. I'm the executor of Orvenia's estate. Vivian Marston's care was being paid for by a trust under Mrs. Colfax's will."

"Do you have any idea why she'd be in Ms. Kendall's basement?"

"No, I'm just as puzzled as you are."

Officer Glover joined them. "I hate to interrupt, but the dispatcher called and said there were several reports of a gray-haired woman dressed in a bathrobe walking down Highway 28."

"What does that have to do with this?" Colleen asked haughtily.

"Mrs. Marston is wearing a bathrobe," Katherine noted.

"And to fill you in, Dan, Mrs. Marston was reported missing from the nursing home at seven. Did the dispatcher mention that?" the chief asked irritably. "It's close to ten now."

"Let me get this straight," Colleen began. "A woman, in a coma, woke up and left the nursing home, in this freezing weather, dressed only in a robe, walked down the highway, came over to this house to specifically die in my friend's basement. Oh, please," she said skeptically.

"The Erie Convalescent Home is only a few blocks north of here," Mark added.

Colleen frowned and stared at the ceiling.

"Chief London, Mrs. Marston has been very ill for the last several weeks," Katherine began. "I know this is probably ridiculous, but when I was growing up, I had a cat named Bruce."

The chief put up his hand, "I don't have time for this."

"Please, hear me out."

"All right, but make it quick," he demanded.

"Bruce was an outside cat. When I was a child, my parents and I lived in Brooklyn. One day a car hit Bruce. My mother saw it happen from the front window. When she ran to the front door and opened it, Bruce staggered in and collapsed on the living room carpet. That's where he died."

Mark gave a curious look. "Do you think that Vivian Marston knew she was dying and wanted to die in this house?"

"Could be," Katherine said. "Didn't you say she loved this house?"

"For pity's sake. The woman was incapacitated," Colleen said to the chief and then to Katherine, "*Now* do you want to stay in this house? I vote we get out of here as soon as possible."

"No, ma'am," the chief said. "I'm afraid I'm going to ask the two of you to remain in the county for at least seventy-two hours."

"With all due respect, you can't ask them to remain in the county unless you think they are suspects," Mark protested.

"Mr. Dunn," the chief began. "I don't need to quote the law to you, but Vivian Marston's death occurred in an unusual manner. The coroner is already here, and I've notified the Indiana State Police."

"This is ridiculous," Katherine protested. "I can't leave the house for seventy-two hours?"

"Maybe less. It depends when the coroner's report is in," the chief answered as he started to leave the room. He looked at Katherine and said, "You can leave the house, but just don't leave the Erie area. Anyway, you weren't planning on leaving us so soon. You just got here."

"No."

"Good. We'll get this thing sorted out."

"Chief, I think you're making a mistake," Mark said slowly.

"Whatever happened under this roof, happened under *her* roof," the chief snapped. "I'm not going to say

Miss Kendall is a suspect until I know more, but she and her friend are material witnesses at least."

"Incredible," Colleen said under her breath. "This makes absolutely no sense. We've been at the blasted movie all night. Why would we want to harm the poor woman?"

The chief clumped down the stairs.

Mark turned to Katherine and said, "How do you think Vivian got in the house?"

"I think Vivian let herself in with the new key," Katherine said suspiciously.

"What do you mean?"

"The chief found a key on the basement floor close to Vivian's body."

"I did *not* give Vivian a duplicate key to your house," Mark said tenaciously. "So, where's the key now?"

"The chief put it in an evidence bag. Listen, I'm not positive it was a new key to the house because he wouldn't let me compare it with my key. Oh, by the way. Who did you hire to change the locks?"

"Why do you ask?"

"Well, try this out for size," Katherine began sarcastically. "The strange thing about this old house is that doors become locked and unlocked by themselves. It's a long story and I'm really too tired to tell it now, but one question—whom did you hire to change the locks?"

"Cokey Cokenberger, of course."

Colleen and Katherine exchanged doubtful looks.

"Seriously?" Katherine asked, shocked. "The handyman changed the locks and not a professional locksmith?"

"I bought the locksets from a locksmith in the city, and I hired Cokey to install them. He's done this sort of work for me before."

"Okay, fine," Katherine said, throwing up her arms in exasperation. "I know I'm jumping to conclusions. Maybe that key the chief found doesn't fit the new door locks, but I want to feel secure in this house. I don't relish getting up in the morning and finding another escapee from the convalescent home *dead* in the basement."

"Hear, hear," Colleen agreed.

"Where are the cats?" Mark asked, changing the subject.

"In the bedroom at the back of the hall," Katherine answered.

"Would you prefer if I stayed here tonight?" Mark offered. "I can sleep in the sitting room."

"Yes, that would be grand," Colleen readily accepted.

"No, thank you," Katherine said stubbornly. "We can fend for ourselves."

"Okay, in that case I'll go now," Mark said. "But first I want to have a word with the chief before I leave. I'll call you first thing tomorrow morning."

Katherine did not answer.

Colleen said, "Thanks. You've been a wonderful help." She elbowed Katherine in the ribs.

"Oh yes, thanks," Katherine stuttered. "I'm sorry, but this whole thing has brought my New York up."

"New York up?" he asked quizzically.

"It's like a cat's fur rising when it's angry. Well, to me, that's my New York. I've got my fur up. And I'm not going to let this deter me," she said adamantly.

Mark said good night and left.

The two women discussed how they would move pieces of furniture to barricade the exterior doors. "We'll start with the side covered carport door," Katherine said, running down the stairs.

"Wait, stop," Colleen said. "What was that business about staying in Erie? What did that mean? I can't go back to New York?" Colleen worried. "How would I explain that to my boss-from-hell? While I was on vacation, I was a suspect for murder! Gee, that really increases my chances of getting a raise. What about my date with Mario?" she continued.

"I don't know what to think. For now, let's start barricading the outside doors so we can call it a day. I'm exhausted."

Colleen descended the stairs. "Later, when we go to bed, can you keep your door closed?"

"Why?" Katherine asked.

"Because those furry creatures of yours might—"

Katherine cut her off. "I promise to keep my door closed, if you keep yours closed."

"And, another thing, why didn't you mention to the chief that my room was vandalized? And my EMF meter was broken?"

"Because I didn't want the chief to think we're nuts. No worries. I'll order you one online, and by the time you get home, you'll have it for your next ghost-hunting adventure."

"Thanks, Katz."

"And I beg of you, if you see something spooky or hear something that goes bump in the night, do not scream," Katherine warned. "I've had enough drama for one evening."

"I'll pull the covers over my head and ignore it."

"Perfect," Katherine said, rolling the letter R. "We're getting giddy."

"I vote for tea."

"I second the motion."

Heading to the kitchen, Colleen said, "I change my vote to a pint of Guinness."

"A glass of wine would be great," Katherine said. She gazed out the slats of the window blind and looked at the ambulance parked outside.

"What's going on?" Colleen asked, pouring the wine. She slid a glass across the table to Katherine.

"They're loading Mrs. Marston into the ambulance. There's this stocky guy standing next to the chief. I wonder if he's the coroner. Oops," Katherine said, stepping back from the window.

"What now?"

"I think the chief saw me looking out."

"So? It's your house. Well, not yet, but in the future." Colleen sat down and poured a bottle of Guinness into a tall glass. "You were awfully tough on Mr. Lawyer this evening. I think you hurt his feelings."

"Colleen, I know you mean well, but I'm not up to another relationship so soon after Gary dumped me for another woman. I'm being very cautious. Besides, Mark was talking out of both sides of his mouth, as the estate's attorney and as my attorney, even though I never hired him."

"Yeah, you're right," Colleen agreed.

They heard the ambulance pull out of the drive. A moment later, they heard two car doors slam and an engine start up. Katherine went back over to the window blinds and sneaked a look outside. "There goes the chief," she said, stepping back.

Colleen popped up beside her and peered through the slats. "Hey, there's another car pulling in."

"What kind of car?"

"It's white with a blue emblem on it. Oh, the saints preserve us, there's a woman coming this way."

"Which door?"

"The side door."

Katherine rushed to the carport door and opened it before the woman had an opportunity to clang the antique doorbell.

"Ms. Kendall," the woman said, somewhat surprised.

"Yes," Katherine answered, not moving from the doorway.

"My name is Detective Linda Martin. I'm an investigator for the Indiana State Police," she said, showing her badge. "I'll be assisting the County Coroner in assessing Mrs. Marston's cause of death. Could I please have a few words with you? I know you must be exhausted from this trying experience, but I'll try not to take up too much of your time."

"Come in," Katherine said, motioning her into the dining room.

"This is truly a beautiful house. I understand you've only lived here a brief time."

"Yes, since Sunday evening," Katherine said. "How may I help you?"

"I heard you're from New York. This death that occurred in your basement—"

Katherine interrupted, "I lived in Brooklyn for most of my life. I've lived in Manhattan for the last few years, but never—I repeat—never have I found a dead body in my basement or anywhere else."

"Out here we have an organization known as the Welcome Patrol. I'm sorry that your welcoming had to be so unpleasant."

Katherine nodded. "Waugh," Scout called loudly from the upstairs guest room. Katherine could hear the Siamese trotting back and forth on the floor above.

The detective looked up. "Is that your baby crying?"

"She's sort of a baby. She's my cat. Actually, she's a Siamese and she's very vocal," Katherine explained.

The detective smiled. "I need to ask you the names of the people who, to your knowledge, have been in this house today. The chief told me that you've kept Orvenia Colfax's small staff. Cokey Cokenberger is your handyman, and Patricia Marston is your yard and garden person. I know that Cokey did some work for you yesterday."

"How do you know that?" Katherine asked curiously.

"You see, Ms. Kendall . . ."

"Please call me Katherine," she said.

Detective Martin continued, "When Cokey saw your house lit up like a Christmas tree, he walked over to check things out. I talked to him a few minutes ago."

"Okay. Sorry, please go on. Would you like to sit in the parlor?"

"No, this is fine," the detective said, sitting down. She opened up her laptop computer. "I like to keep up with technology," she said, "So, if you don't mind my typing your answers, we can begin."

Katherine drew up a chair and sat next to her; Colleen came into the room from the kitchen, but remained standing. Katherine introduced. "Detective, this is my friend Colleen. She was with me when we found Vivian's body."

"Hello," the detective greeted. "I'm pleased to meet you. As I was just saying to Katherine, I'll try to keep this as brief as possible."

Colleen nodded.

"Was Patricia Marston here today?" Detective Martin asked.

"No, but according to my attorney, Mark Dunn, Patricia brought over some baked goods on Sunday before we arrived."

"So, no one other than your friend and you were home today?"

"Yes, that's correct, but we weren't home *all* day. We left this morning to go to the city and didn't get home until later."

"And when was that?"

Colleen interjected, "It was getting dark. We hurriedly unloaded the car, and then we went to the movie."

"Here in town?"

"Yes."

"When you went to the theater, did you leave any of the exterior doors unlocked?"

"I checked the doors on the first floor, but I didn't check the walk-out basement door," Katherine answered.

"And why was that?" the detective asked.

"Well, because my friend and I were down there yesterday afternoon and made sure it was locked. Cokey had done some work for me and left by that door. Colleen and I wanted to make sure he'd turned the lock in the knob when he went home," Katherine explained.

"When you left the house to go to the movie, which door did you use?"

"We went out that way," Katherine said, pointing to the side carport door.

"Okay, so you went to see a movie. What time did you leave the theater?" the detective asked.

"Nine something," Katherine said. Colleen nodded in agreement.

"Chief London mentioned you had vandals in your bedroom. What do you think they were looking for?"

"I don't have a clue. There isn't anything of interest in there. I'd unpacked my suitcases—just clothing and some of my cats' stuff."

"Was anything stolen?"

"No," Katherine answered.

"Do you have any idea where your cats were when the bedroom was ransacked? Cokey told me that yesterday one of your cats overturned heavy flowerpots; do you think your cat could also rummage through a room?"

Katherine shook her head. "No, I don't think it's possible," she said.

"One time my tiger tabbies—you see, I have two—thought they were racing in the Indy 500 and knocked my computer off the desk," Detective Martin continued.

Katherine thought for a moment and then dismissed the idea. "I know my cats aren't capable of pulling clothes off hangers and piling them in the middle of the floor, or flinging a heavy mattress off the bed."

"The chief said when he initially searched the house, your bedroom door was locked. Can I assume you had locked the cats inside?"

"Well, no," Katherine said. "When Colleen and I returned from the movie and came inside the house, my cats were downstairs, which was strange because before we left, we'd shut them in my bedroom. But I didn't lock them in there. I just assumed the chief had let them out when he checked the room."

"If only cats could talk," the detective offered. "Sometimes these old doors have skeleton keys you can use to lock them from the outside."

Katherine shrugged and said, "I think the vandal, or whoever, heard the chief coming up the stairs, hid in my bedroom and locked the door. The chief said he heard my cats; they knew a stranger was in the room and they wanted out. When the chief left, the vandal made his way out of the room and shut the door behind him, which is how I found it."

"You seem to be reliving it," Detective Martin observed suspiciously.

"What can I say? I watch a lot of CSI reruns. But I'm telling you, this jerk was upstairs when the chief was here, sneaked down the back stairs, which feeds into the kitchen, and then turned the corner and exited via my office door, which by the way, was bolt-locked when I left for the movie, yet was unlocked when Officer Glover later found it," Katherine said breathlessly.

"Actually, we think your vandal was one or possibly two locals who have done this kind of thing before. Within the last month, there have been three break-ins with a similar type of vandalism, where nothing is stolen, but the house's contents are turned upside-down. You're lucky you called the police when you did."

"May I ask what their motive is?"

"Fun and games . . . who knows?" the detective said.

"This may be a long shot," Katherine began, "but do you think the vandals went down to the basement and frightened Vivian?"

"Why do you suspect that?"

"Because there weren't any apparent marks on Vivian to indicate her cause of death—"

"Are you a coroner?" the detective asked.

"No, but maybe the vandals scared Vivian to death. I know if I came upon people that didn't belong in the house, I'd totally freak out."

"I'll make a note of that," the detective said, keying in the information. When she finished, she looked up and asked, "Who has keys to your house?"

"Just me. Before I arrived on Sunday, my attorney had the locks changed."

"Are you *sure*?" Detective Martin inquired.

"Yes, why do you ask?"

"Is there any reason Vivian Marston would have a key to your house?"

"If she had one, it would be the older key for the locks before they were changed."

"I'll put it this way. The key the chief found on your basement floor fits the new locks."

"And the plot thickens," Katherine muttered under her breath.

"After we processed the key for prints, I tried it on three of your exterior doors. And guess what? Not only does it fit, but it works. Now, I'll ask you again, did you give a duplicate of your new set of keys to anyone else?"

"Absolutely not," Katherine said defensively. "You need to talk to Cokey Cokenberger. He's the one who changed the locks. Maybe he didn't read the memo that said no one but me was to have a key."

"I'll talk to him. Well, that's about the extent of it," Detective Martin said, snapping her laptop shut. "I'll call you if I have any more questions," she said. "And if you think of anything else, call me at this number." She handed Katherine a business card.

"Sure," Katherine said.

"Waugh," Scout protested upstairs.

"Better see to your cat," the detective said, leaving. "Oh, yes. I locked your basement outside door, but I suggest you go through the house and double check the locks." She closed the side door, which squeaked on its hinges behind her.

Katherine sighed and said to Colleen, "I'm glad that's over."

"She seems friendly enough, but she's definitely suspicious of you."

"Great, that is just great. You were awfully quiet," Katherine noted.

"I was just trying to figure out why she kept asking questions about the key. She needs to be talking to Mr. Handy Dandy man. It doesn't make sense that he would give the new key to the housekeeper when she's in a coma at the convalescent home," Colleen said skeptically, then added, "I mean the now deceased housekeeper." She made the sign of the cross.

"I don't know how that poor woman got into this house," Katherine sighed. "Maybe Cokey misunderstood Mark's instructions and made a copy for Vivian, her daughter, and himself," she said, frustrated.

"Maybe this and maybe that, Katz. She had to get in the house somehow. But what about Scout's behavior? I'm not a cat person, but do cats normally act like that?"

Katherine shook her head. "Not thinkin' so. I've seen Scout arch her back and hop up and down, but I've never seen her do that strange dance before."

"She was screeching like a wild animal."

"I thought that was strange too."

"Katz, why didn't you tell the detective about the electricity being deliberately turned off?"

"Because she made that comment that I was *reliving it*, like I did it. Besides, it doesn't make any sense. None of this makes any sense."

"Well, it certainly does to me," Colleen said tartly. "Someone murdered poor Mrs. Marston."

"Why do you say that?"

"Have you forgotten the bag with the foot sticking out from under it? You cannot convince me that a woman on her death bed covered herself up with a plastic bag and then died by the water heater, of all places."

"You don't need to convince me," Katherine said, pulling a heavy Eastlake chair and barricading the dining room door. "Something is not right here."

"It's been a terrible day. Let's do what the detective said. Let's lock up and get some sleep. I'll help you make up your bed."

"Sounds like a plan," Katherine said wearily.

Chapter Eight

A thin ray of sunlight filtered through the leaded glass transom over the tall window of the guest room. Katherine shifted uncomfortably on the lumpy mattress. She adjusted the feather pillow and lay back down. She admired the gold-edged ceiling medallion and the rose-colored glass of the chandelier. She heard a slight noise from the top of the massive, ornate headboard. Her eyes followed the sound to its source, atop the broad triangular pediment on the headboard's peak. "Abby," she said, surprised. "How did you get up there?"

"Chirp," Abby replied, as she launched herself from the pediment and, with paws held out like a dive off the highboard, soared five feet down to the mattress below. "Chir-r-r-p," she trilled and began to purr. Katherine petted her.

"You little rascal," Katherine said, moving her closer and kissing her. She scanned the room for the other cats. "Lilac," she called.

There was a slight movement inside the heavy velvet curtains—the Scottish lace panel moved to one side—and a Siamese head popped out, "Me-yowl." She was sitting on the top rail of the window's bottom sash.

"Why can't you be an ordinary cat and sit on the windowsill?"

Lilac turned, dug her front claws into the lace panel curtain, dropped her rear feet off the top of the window sash, and swung her body down to hang, like Tarzan, from the curtain.

"Lilac, no. You'll tear it," Katherine scolded.

Lilac twisted her body from the outside of the curtain to the inside, descended unevenly to the bottom windowsill for a fraction of a second, and with renewed confidence sprang effortlessly from the sill onto the bed. She immediately started to wash Abigail's ears.

Iris was sitting on the antique dresser, leaning over and watching Scout on the floor. Scout was making tiny *waugh* noises in rapid succession and was busy digging for something under the bed.

"Stop that, Scout," Katherine said sleepily. "I want to go back to sleep."

Katherine heard something fall beneath. "What was that?" she asked, sitting bolt upright. She peered over the side of the bed and observed Scout's rump and tail. She was wedged halfway under the side rail. Her thumping tail was flipping like a pendulum in acute feline concentration. "Get out of there," Katherine demanded.

Scout backed out clutching a small, leather-bound book in her jaws. Her brown mask was covered with cobwebs.

"Put that down," Katherine ordered.

"Waugh," Scout said, dropping it. Scout sneezed and then made smacking noises with her tongue.

Katherine hastened out of bed and picked up Scout. She brushed the cobwebs off her face, then took a look inside Scout's mouth to make sure she hadn't swallowed anything. She set her down. "You can't taste a book by its cover." Scout ran over to the water dish and began lapping up water.

Katherine picked up the book and started to read the title out loud: "What to Do," and stopped abruptly, "in Cases of Poisoning."

There was a loud knock on the door. Iris growled. Lilac and Abigail laid their ears back and stood to attention. Scout raced to the door—a droplet of water on her nose—ready to fling out. "Katz, are you okay?" Colleen said on the other side.

Katherine opened the door. "You won't believe what Scout just found under the bed."

"Looks like an old book," Colleen said, then sneezed.

Katherine opened the torn binding. "It's ancient, all right. It was published in 1897."

"How about a bit of breakfast?" Colleen asked, starting to leave.

"Wait a second," Katherine exclaimed. "The section on arsenic is underlined."

"What's this book about?"

"Poisoning."

"Who do you think it belonged to? Is there a name inside?"

Katherine flipped through several pages. "None that I can see."

"It's a strange book to be under the bed. Who stayed in this room?"

"When Mark first took me through the house, he said this was the main guest room. After my great aunt died, Vivian Marston slept here."

"Some guest room," Colleen said in awe. "The stuff in here has to be priceless. It's almost like you could take everything in here and move it to one of those period rooms at the Metropolitan Museum of Art. Just look at the headboard with the gargoyle carved on it—"

"Cherub," Katherine corrected.

"I bet that bed has been in the same spot since 1897. It's too big and heavy to move anywhere else. Katz, the book could belong to anybody. What's the name of the book?"

"*What to do in Cases of Poisoning* by William Murrell."

Colleen's eyes got big. "Maybe the housekeeper found out your great aunt was going to cut her out of the will, so she studied this book to figure out how to kill the old lady."

"You've been reading too much Agatha Christie."

"Waugh," Scout cried insistently. She had returned to the room and had placed one paw on Katherine's foot. "Waugh," she begged.

Katherine put the book on the dresser, then picked up Scout. "The book seems to be a medical book on what to do if someone is poisoned, not a guide on how to murder someone. And, besides, my great aunt didn't cut her out of the will."

"Do you realize every time I come up with an idea, Scout gets all bent out of shape?" Colleen sniffed.

"Pay no mind to Scout. She's probably hungry," Katherine chuckled. "Allow me to get this straight. You think Vivian Marston poisoned my great aunt so she'd inherit everything? Mark said my great aunt's will created a $200,000 trust for her. That's a nice pocket of change for a housekeeper, don't ya think?"

"Poor woman doesn't collect a dime because she ends up dying in your basement," Colleen noted. "On second thought, on television they exhume bodies and check for poisoning," Colleen offered.

"Waugh." Scout leaped from Katherine's arms and landed on the bed.

"Arsenic is a regulated substance. How would Vivian Marston get a hold of it? Besides, my great aunt died of a massive coronary. I've watched enough TV to know that dying of arsenic poisoning is a cruel, prolonged process."

"Oh, well," Colleen shrugged. "It was just something that popped into my head. My theory is that the housekeeper went daft, overexerted herself walking over here, then died of a heart attack. I'm sure the coroner will determine she died of natural causes."

"For our sake, I hope so," Katherine agreed. "Do you think it's possible that Vivian, in some sort of delirium, tore up my bedroom?"

"Waugh. Waugh," Scout said, butting her head into Katherine's leg.

"I don't think so, Katz. I wouldn't have the strength to create such a disaster. And the housekeeper in her state couldn't have done it, either."

"Maybe that's how she overexerted herself," Katherine continued.

"But what was she searching for?"

"I don't have a clue."

"'Tis a mystery. By the way, did you ever read the entire will?"

"No, Mark never sent me the rest of it. I'm going to request a hard copy."

"That's a bit odd. Maybe there's something in there he doesn't want you to see," Colleen said suspiciously.

"Oh, he just forgot."

"I can't help but wonder who else benefited from the will besides you."

"All I know is that a $200,000 trust was set up for Vivian, but I don't know the details. Last night, Mark mentioned to the chief that my great aunt's estate or the trust was paying Mrs. Marston's medical expenses."

"Waugh," Scout demanded, nipping Katherine's leg.

"Ouch," she cried. "Bad cat."

"Maybe Scout is on to something."

"Yeah, my leg."

"Look, look behind you," Colleen said excitedly, pointing to the dresser.

Scout had leaped up onto the marble top and was clutching the poison book in her teeth. Her sapphire blue eyes were crossed, and she seemed to be in some sort of feline state of euphoria.

"Gimme that," Katherine demanded.

Scout dropped the book and shot off of the dresser. She rounded the corner and bounded loudly down the hall.

"Come back here!"

"Katz, that's it. Vivian Marston was looking for the book but she was searching in the *wrong* room," Colleen exclaimed. "Scout should be helping the police."

"Scout is a known drug addict. I've caught her licking the processing fluid off old photographs, slurping the tops of household cleanser cans, and once, she ate a fabric softener sheet."

"I've never heard of a junkie cat."

"Most likely there's a chemical in the book binding that Scout wants to get high on," Katherine said, opening the top drawer and putting the book inside. "You know what really unnerves me?"

"What, that your cat needs to enter a drug rehab center?"

"No, that my inner sanctum has been violated. I'm desperate to know who ransacked my room, and I don't believe for a moment that a bunch of local hooligans did it."

"I have another notion in my head, that perhaps this house has a poltergeist," Colleen ventured.

"Oh, please. You don't really think this house is haunted?"

"Well, now," Colleen said, with her hands on her hips. "Considering the fact my ghost meter has been smashed into smithereens, I can't very well find out."

"And, I *am* so sorry about that," Katherine said.

"Something happened last night. Actually, in the middle of the night, because it woke me up from a dead sleep," Colleen began. "It sounded like something was scratching on my door."

"It couldn't have been the cats because they were locked up with me all night."

"I know. That's why I didn't get up and answer it."

"Maybe it was a tree limb outside, or something rattling on the street."

"I looked," Colleen said. "Katz, come here." She directed Katherine to the hallway back window. "Look out. There isn't a tree to be seen, and the street is in front of the house."

"I didn't hear anything."

"Of course not. You're legally dead when you sleep."

"But if there is something odd, the cats always wake me up."

"Maybe this time they didn't."

"I bet you're going to tell me that the ghost of Vivian Marston tapped on your door last night."

"The saints preserve us," Colleen said theatrically, covering her ears. "It's not right to speak about the newly departed."

"The saints preserve us," Katherine imitated, covering her ears. "Five seconds ago, you thought I should dig up my great aunt."

"Waugh," Scout wailed.

In the guest room, one of the cats began coughing and gagging.

Katherine darted back into the room and found Abigail hunched over on the Renaissance bed. "Abby?"

"What's wrong?" Colleen said, rushing in behind her.

Abigail continued retching and then threw up a large beige hairball. She glanced at Katherine as if she didn't understand what had happened. Katherine picked her up and said, "Does your tummy hurt, sweetheart?" Abigail squeezed her eyes.

"Is she going to be okay?" Colleen asked, hovering nearby. "Oh, the saints preserve us."

"Preserve us again? Now what's wrong?"

"Look at my best cable-knit sweater," Colleen said, holding up last night's cat nest, which now bore a large, gaping hole in the neck. "The little terror tried to eat my sweater."

"Chirp," Abigail hiccupped guiltily. The Abyssinian squirmed free of Katherine's grasp, jumped off the bed, and scampered down the hall.

Katherine stooped down and re-examined the hairball. "It's wool," she said.

"So?" Colleen said, eyes blazing.

"Abigail must have a wool fetish."

"A what?"

"Pica is an unnatural craving for non-food substances. I've read that Siamese sometimes develop a liking for wool, but I didn't know other cats did, as well."

Iris growled.

"What's the matter?"

The front door bell rang loudly. Katherine put on her robe and raced down the stairs, as the bell clanged a second time. "Okay, already. I'm coming." She rushed to the door and opened it.

"Interstate Shipping," said a man dressed in an olive-green uniform, stamping his feet to rid them of slush.

"Yes?" Katherine asked, observing the panel truck parked on the street.

"Are you Ms. Kendall?"

"Yes. Yes. Are you delivering my boxes from New York?"

He looked down at his notebook and nodded. "I need you to sign on these lines." He handed her a plastic pen.

Katherine signed and handed the notebook back to him.

"They're a total of twenty boxes. Is there a way to wedge open this door?"

"I'll let you in and out. I have cats."

He rushed back to his truck.

"Who is it?" Colleen called over the upstairs handrail.

"Some guy delivering my boxes, in the dead of winter, not wearing a coat."

"I'll be right down."

"Bring my fuzzy slippers."

The first box unloaded was Katherine's desktop computer. She clapped her hands gleefully. The man loaded the CPU and monitor boxes onto a hand-truck and managed it up the porch steps. "Where to?" he asked.

"Please come inside. I'll show you after I close the door."

Colleen came down and handed Katherine her slippers.

The deliveryman looked around and complimented, "I love old houses. This is the neatest house I've ever seen."

Katherine put her slippers on and showed the man to her new office. He set down the box and returned to the truck for another one. The cats became hyperactive and began running around the house.

After he delivered all of the boxes, she thanked him and suggested that he wear a coat. He grinned and left.

"Let's get the computer hooked up first. Email, Internet, our link to the outside world," Colleen said dramatically.

"Hold on there, Missy. The cable company gave us a window from ten to noon."

"We can still get everything set up."

"I'm good with that." Then added, "I don't know what I was thinking. Some of these boxes go upstairs. Why did I make that poor man bring them all back here?"

"Point them out and I'll carry them up there."

"Some of them are really heavy."

"No problem," Colleen said. "I'll be fine unless one of your creatures trips me."

"I'm going to get dressed first."

"I'll make some tea."

* * * *

By early afternoon, most of the boxes were unpacked. The computer was on the antique desk along with the printer, but Katherine had to forage in one of the other rooms for a table to set the scanner on. She found an Eastlake table that didn't have a marble top, and moved a Waterford crystal vase from the table to the fireplace mantel. Colleen helped move a damask-covered wing chair to serve as an office chair.

By 11:30, the Colfax mansion had something it had never had — high-speed Internet service. The moment the cable technician left, Colleen said impatiently, "Now, can I pull my email?"

"Yes, by all means," Katherine said, struggling to get out of the chair. "But this wing back is not working for me. My back is killing me."

"I don't care. Move over," Colleen said, adjusting the chair. "After I get done, you can order a proper office chair online," she giggled.

As Colleen was logging into her email account, she became pensive and said, "I don't want to upset you, but don't you think we've had rotten luck since we left Manhattan?"

"I know," Katherine said sadly. "I just had such a wonderful daydream of how happy I'd be here, but then Vivian Marston dies in the basement."

225

"Don't kick yourself too hard, Katz. It wasn't your fault. It wasn't my fault. It's just something dreadful that happened."

"Look, while you're doing that, I'll go up to my vandalized room and see what I can do with it," Katherine said, leaving. From the next room, she called back to Colleen, "Hey, before I forget, Mark texted me a while back and said we deserved a pizza night. So, he's picking us up at 7:00."

"Got it," Colleen said. "Tell me true. Is there really a place in this town that makes pizza?"

"I guess so," Katherine laughed and walked into the atrium. Iris darted after her and nearly tripped her.

"Iris, are you trying to kill me?"

The little cat growled, and then the doorbell rang.

Racing to the front door, Katherine opened it to find Patricia Marston standing outside. "Patricia," Katherine said, surprised.

"May I come in?" Patricia asked tentatively.

"Yes, of course. Please come in," Katherine said, directing Patricia into the parlor. "I think the chairs in here are the most comfortable ones in the entire house."

Patricia sat down.

Iris hunkered in. Her ears were twitching nervously. Patricia tried to pet her, but Iris emitted a low growl and dodged behind the chair.

"Iris, be nice," Katherine warned.

Iris slunk back and warily eyed Patricia. She drew her gums back and exposed her fangs. "Hissss," she snarled menacingly.

"Iris!" Katherine scolded. She turned to Patricia and apologized. "I don't know what has gotten into her."

"I don't like the way that cat is looking at me," Patricia said nervously.

Katherine quickly moved to pick up the hostile cat. When she reached down to snatch Iris, the Siamese squirmed from her grasp and bulleted out of the room. She partially hid behind the Eastlake hall tree and watched intently from her corner vantage point. From where Katherine was standing in the parlor, she could observe Iris's tail thrashing back and forth angrily.

"I'm so sorry about your mother," Katherine said solemnly. "If there's anything I can do, please let me know."

"Can you think of any reason why my mother was in your house last night?" Patricia asked sharply, and with sudden energy.

"No, quite frankly, I can't," Katherine said sitting down. "Would you care for some tea or coffee?"

"No, this isn't a social visit. I'm quite upset that my mother chose to wake up from a coma and die in your house. This is totally unacceptable to me."

"Actually, it's quite unacceptable to me as well," Katherine countered.

"My mother slaved for Orvenia Colfax for thirty long years. That old bag promised this house to her. Now they're both dead and *you're* living here," Patricia said coldly.

"I'm truly sorry about your loss, but I don't appreciate your tone," Katherine said, getting up. "I think you'd better leave now."

"Everything was fine until you showed up!" Patricia got up and started for the door. "If any of Mother's belongings are still here, please call and let me know so I can make arrangements to pick them up."

Katherine walked into the vestibule and opened the door.

On the way out, Patricia turned her head to reveal tears welling in her eyes. In a quavering voice, but with increasing anger, she said, "Under the circumstances, I choose not to work for you. Thank you and good day." She walked briskly from the house and started to get in her car.

"Wait," Katherine called after her. "Do you have a key to my house?"

Patricia gave a haughty look. "I don't have a key to your house. I never had a key to your house." She slammed the car door and started the engine. Katherine closed the door.

Iris came out from hiding and bumped into Katherine's leg. "Yowl," she said, looking up with innocent eyes.

"Yowl, indeed. What's with that make-the-guest-uncomfortable routine? I don't think I want to see that again, Miss Siam," she admonished.

Iris slithered into the living room with her head down.

Katherine called after her. "And no pouting either. Your human has lived in this house for a few days, and already she's had a woman die in the basement, a burglar who didn't steal anything, a best friend who claims she's seen a ghost, and an employee—who baked delicious muffins and minded the plants—quit without notice. Your little act didn't help much."

"Yowl," Iris sassed.

"Hey, Katz," Colleen yelled. "Did I hear you talking to someone?"

Katherine went into the office. "You missed an incredible amount of drama."

"What?" Colleen said, logging off the computer. "Who was at the door?"

"Patricia Marston."

"Patricia? That poor woman. She must be beside herself with grief."

"I'd say more like beside herself with anger. She quit! Take a look at the new gardener," Katherine said pointing to herself.

"Get out!" Colleen said in amazement.

"Not only did she quit, but she also demanded that if we find anything that belonged to her mother, we should notify her so she can make arrangements to pick them up."

"Did she give you a reason why she was quitting?"

"No, I didn't ask her. She wasn't exactly friendly."

"Katz, she just lost her mother."

"Okay. Okay. I feel rotten."

"Did you ask her if her mother was missing a poison book?" Colleen asked cynically.

"For heaven's sake, Colleen. You're being silly. The woman started out meek and depressed, then nearly bit my head off. I wasn't about to ask such a question."

Colleen stifled a laugh.

"Besides, there's a hole in your theory."

"Sort of like the hole in my sweater?"

"The book Scout found is ancient. Surely Vivian Marston could have found a more up-to-date book," Katherine said.

"Oh, please Katz, let's not go there again."

"Did you get any interesting email?" Katherine asked, changing the subject.

"Well, after deleting tons of junk mail, I found one from Jacky quite interesting. He said that my stuff has been moved to the apartment, and that he already finished putting up the partition in the living room."

"Wow, that was quick."

"I'll have my own room and Jacky will have his. This will be the first time for the both of us. I'm so excited about having my own place."

Katherine suddenly looked depressed.

"I'm sorry, Katz," Colleen apologized. "Are you homesick?"

"No, it's not that. I'm just somewhat sad that my stay here has been so dramatic. It was hell to drive out here. Now it's turning out to be hell to live here. I've always been so honest all my life. It saddens me that anyone could possibly think I was a party to Vivian Marston's death."

"Cheer up," Colleen consoled. "Look, I'm finished here. Let's go upstairs and tackle your new bedroom."

"Considering what happened last night, I don't think I'll ever sleep in that room again."

"But, why?" Colleen raised her eyebrows curiously.

"Bad vibes, that's all."

"Waugh," Scout agreed.

"And Scout, are you getting bad vibes too?" Colleen joked.

The two went upstairs with Scout and Iris bringing up the rear.

* * * *

Mark arrived a few minutes past seven and parked behind Katherine's Toyota. He quickly got out of his car and rushed up the carport steps. He clanged the brass doorbell twice and Colleen answered.

"Hey," he said cheerily.

"Hello," Colleen answered. "Her Royal Highness is not ready yet, so would you like to come in for a minute until she blesses us with—"

"I heard that, Carrot Top," Katherine said as she descended the stairs. "Hi, Mark. Thanks so much for inviting us to dinner tonight. I hope you don't mind two starving women. We've been working all day, and quite frankly, I could eat an entire pie."

232

Mark laughed. "Let's head to the hotel."

"Wait a minute! Did you say hotel?" Katherine asked.

"Yes, the Erie Hotel makes the best pizzas."

"Isn't there another restaurant?"

"Why?" he asked, and then added, "They don't make you wear a bib if you order pizza."

Colleen asked, "Doesn't Patricia Marston work there?"

"Yes, but she most likely won't be working there tonight. I'm sure Velma gave her the week off. You shouldn't avoid her just because of last night. You had absolutely nothing to do with her mother's death."

"Patricia came over today and quit."

"What?" Mark asked, shocked. "I'm surprised. She's worked for Orvenia for several years. This was her job during summer vacation. As soon as you get the coroner's report, you can make her a copy, and then maybe she'll come back and work for you."

"Actually, I'm not interested," Katherine said.

"Waugh," Scout protested upstairs.

"I closed the cats up in my room," Katherine said quickly. "The two of you are my witnesses. If we come home tonight and find the cats prowling about, we'll definitely know someone has been coming into the house and playing a game."

"What do you mean?" Mark asked.

"Last night, when the chief searched the house, my bedroom door was closed and locked."

"And?"

"This morning I examined the door. There are two locks on it: one is an old, antique lock which at one time probably had a skeleton key, and the other one is a modern bolt lock—interior bolt lock—without a key. To lock the door, one has to bolt it from the inside."

Colleen became frightened. "Oh, Katz, please don't scare me again."

"So, what you're saying," Mark began, "is that someone was in your room when the chief searched the house? I wonder why he didn't ask you to unlock the door so he could check inside."

"I don't know," Katherine shrugged.

"I can't understand why anyone would want to ransack Orvenia's room. All of her jewelry and valuables have been placed in a lock-box at the bank. Her clothes were donated to charity. She did have a small safe on the closet floor, but after she passed away, I personally removed the contents and put them in my law office's safe."

Katherine was silent for a moment and then said, "Maybe it wasn't a vandal. Maybe the person was looking for something in my room—something belonging to my great aunt."

"Maybe the housekeeper came up here before she died in the basement," Colleen surmised.

"I doubt that. She was very weak," Mark noted. "As a matter of fact, I can't believe she made it out of her bed, let alone walk several blocks down here."

Katherine asked Mark, "While we are on the topic of locks, did you get in touch with Cokey and find out about the key?"

"Actually, I did. And, I apologize for not letting you know earlier. Detective Martin called me and said the key the chief found was a copy of the new house key. She said she already spoke to you about it. So, I got a hold of Cokey. He said he kept the second key of the locksets because he needed to get in and out of the house while you were still in New York. He's very sorry. He said the key must have fallen out of his pocket the previous day."

"I guess that makes sense," Katherine said. "So how do I get my key back?"

"Probably not until the coroner's ruling is in."

Colleen flipped her red hair back and said nonchalantly, "Are we going to be discussing this topic very long? I'm starving."

"Yes, I'm starving, too," Mark said. "After you, Ladies," he said politely.

The three headed for the restaurant. When they arrived, they were shocked to see Patricia working.

"Are you sure you two want to stay?" Mark asked.

"I'm good. Let's just get through it," Katherine said.

Velma Richardson bustled over and seated them in a quiet section of the dining room. She said to Katherine, "I remember you. You wanted some kind of wine and I didn't know what it was."

"I hope I didn't embarrass you."

"Shoot no," Velma said, winking. "Do you want that Caber tonight?"

"Yes, please."

"Do you have a beer menu?" Colleen asked mischievously.

Katherine smirked.

"No, but I can tell ya what we have. Bud, Bud Light, and Amstel Light."

"No Guinness," Colleen said, scrunching up her face.

"Just what I named ya."

"Okay, bring me an Amstel Light."

"Me, too," Mark said.

While Velma was filling their drink orders, they engaged in idle small talk. Mark wanted to know about Abigail's adjustment to the three Siamese. Katherine inquired about the Maine Coon. Colleen told funny stories about the cats, and Mark shared his stories about Bruiser. The conversation was deliberately kept light for reasons that none of them dared say.

Patricia served the drinks and quickly took their pizza order. Katherine asked for a side salad and Patricia listed several salad dressings. "Ranch, Italian, French, Poppy seed . . ."

"Poppy seed?" Katherine asked.

"It's quite good," Mark answered.

"Okay, then. I'll try it."

Patricia briskly walked away, and Colleen began to tap her teeth with a mischievous glint in her eye.

When Patricia brought the salad and set it on the table, Katherine turned up her nose and said, "On second thought I think I'll have the Ranch."

While Patricia reached for the salad, Colleen slid the bowl in front of her. "I'll take it," she said, diving her fork into the lettuce.

Patricia scowled, then said to Katherine, "I'll bring you another one. What kind of dressing did you say?"

"Ranch—like dude ranch?"

Patricia huffed away.

"Katz, this salad dressing is delicious. Are you sure you don't want to try it?"

"No," Katherine said. "The seeds get stuck in my teeth. Remember, Colleen?"

Mark laughed.

"Well, they do," Katherine said.

Colleen chuckled. "What's with these people in Indiana putting poppy seeds into everything? Poppy seed muffins," she began. "Poppy seed salad dressing—"

"Poppy seed pizza," Katherine joked.

"Poppy seed daiquiri," Mark added, joining the name game.

"And for dessert we'll have poppy seed cheesecake." Colleen burst out laughing.

Velma brought over the second salad and explained that she'd be their server. The three were relieved.

The pizza arrived and they ate in silence, occasionally commenting about how good the food was. At nine, Mark drove them home and the three went inside. Nothing seemed unusual. The lights they'd turned on previously were still on, and the cats weren't loitering in the atrium. Mark excused himself, saying he had to drive to Indianapolis in the morning to attend a seminar. After he left, Colleen and Katherine exchanged a few observations regarding the hostile Patricia, then went upstairs. Katherine opened the guest room door and the four cats spilled out.

"Waugh," Scout protested. "Me-yowl," Lilac said. "Chirp," Abby added.

"Iris," Katherine called.

"Yowl," Iris said.

"Nothing seems out of the ordinary," Colleen noted.

"How are my kids?" Katherine asked the cats. "Listen, Colleen, is it okay if I let them roam tonight?"

"I don't mind. They won't bother me anyway. I'll keep my door closed. I'm going to call Mum, and then call it a night."

"Okay, but do you realize what I haven't done yet?"

"What?"

"I haven't checked my email messages."

"Better check them."

Katherine bound down the stairs and went into her office. She was surprised to find her computer on and an image on the screen.

"Colleen," she yelled. "Could you come down here for a minute?"

Colleen came running down. "Where are you?"

"In my office."

Colleen came in. "What's wrong?"

"Look," Katherine said, pointing at the monitor.

"Looks like a Google search."

"Look what's on the screen."

"A book review—Madame Bovine." Colleen squinted to read.

"No, Madame Bovary. It's a book written by a French author. You've never read it?"

"No, can't say that I have."

"The main character died of arsenic poisoning."

Colleen slid down in the wing back chair. "I was searching for office chairs. I must have forgotten to log off. Guilty."

"I'm glad that you didn't log off."

"Why?"

"Because it means Lilac or one of the other cats darted in here and either stepped on the mouse or stood on the keyboard."

Lilac heard her name and trotted into the room. With one powerful push of her back legs, she jumped from the floor to the keyboard. A loud series of beeps began.

"You monkey," Katherine admonished, "have you been surfing the Web?"

Lilac rubbed her throat on the corner of the flat-screen monitor.

"Amazing," Colleen observed.

"My cats are very smart," Katherine said proudly. "But they're not computer literate."

Colleen got up and said, "I'm off to call Mum. Pleasant dreams."

"See you tomorrow," Katherine said as she logged off the Internet. Abby appeared from the back of the monitor. With her right paw, she clicked the mouse. Katherine picked up the Abyssinian and said, "Don't let Colleen see you do that. She'll want to enter you in an amazing pet contest."

Chapter Nine

Katherine was sleeping in a deep, comatose state. She dreamed she was planting flowers in the garden beside the carriage house. Vivian and Patricia Marston stood behind her instructing her about what to do. Great Aunt Orvenia brought out glasses of lemonade and said Katherine needed to take the seeds out of the package before planting. Everyone was happy.

A heavy weight landed on Katherine's chest and abruptly disconnected the dream. "Ouch," Katherine muttered. A cat scurried noisily out of the room.

It's so dark, Katherine thought. She reached over and turned on the bedside lamp and noticed that none of the cats were in the room. *Great*, she thought. *They're probably annoying Colleen by scratching on her door, or engaged in all manner of feline mischief throughout the house.*

She put on her robe and flipped the switch to the overhead chandelier. She squinted across the hall and noticed the bathroom door was ajar. She could see a sliver of light coming from the side. She tapped lightly on the door. "Colleen, are you in there?"

When Colleen didn't answer, Katherine pushed the door open and hurried inside. Colleen was draped over the bathtub.

242

"What's wrong?" Katherine asked.

The four cats silently sat on the bathroom counter, leaning over the edge and peering down at the prostrate woman on the floor below.

"I'm so sick," Colleen said faintly.

"Let's get you back to bed," Katherine said.

"No," Colleen protested. "I'm sick to my stomach."

"I'll get something to put by your bed. You have to get under the covers. It's freezing in here."

"I feel so dizzy. I keep retching and retching and all I can see are those poppy seeds."

"The salad dressing must have been spoiled," Katherine said.

Colleen began retching again.

Katherine touched Colleen's forehead. "You feel incredibly hot."

"I'm burning up and my heart is racing a mile a minute."

"I'm taking you to the hospital."

Katherine retrieved her cell phone and tapped in 911. "I have an emergency. I think my friend has food poisoning. I'm in Erie. Where is the nearest hospital?"

"Want us to send an ambulance?" the man's voice drawled.

"No, just give me the number of the City Hospital."

"You could have called directory assistance for that," he said smugly. "But I'll give it to you anyway." He gave the telephone number to Katherine. She hung up and entered the number. The hospital operator gave her directions. She rushed back to check on Colleen, who was still sprawled over the bathtub.

"I think I'm dying," she said feebly. "I was in my room and a monk appeared and told me I was going to die," she slurred.

"This is nonsense," Katherine said. "You're delirious." She took off her robe and threw it over Colleen. "I'm going to throw something on, get the car started and then I'm coming up for you."

Katherine hastened down the stairs and grabbed her winter coat off the Eastlake hall tree. She put it on as she ran out the side door. She jammed the key in the ignition, but the car didn't respond. The dashboard indicators remained dark. She tried again; the starter wouldn't turn over. She tried a third time; no response. "Dammit," she cursed. She ran back into the house, grabbed a flashlight and returned to the Toyota. She popped the hood and took a quick look to discover that someone had stolen her battery. She let the hood slam shut, called 911 again, and this time requested an ambulance. Within a few minutes, an ambulance pulled into the drive and two attendants got out. Katherine met them at the side door.

"Through this room and up the stairs," Katherine directed.

The two attendants supported Colleen down the stairs. They lifted her up into the ambulance and made her lie down on the gurney.

"Listen, my car won't start. Can I ride with you?" Katherine asked one of the attendants.

"Sure thing," the closest one said.

When the driver started to back out the driveway, he yelled back, "Which hospital?"

"The one in the city," Katherine answered.

"But that's farther away. There's a hospital just over the bridge."

"I didn't know. Okay, let's go there."

The driver turned on the flashing lights and they sped out of Erie.

"How are you feeling now?" Katherine asked Colleen.

"Horrible," she moaned.

The ambulance pulled in front of the Emergency Room and a nurse met them at the door.

"Number Two is available," the nurse directed.

The ambulance attendants lifted the gurney out of the bus and wheeled Colleen into the small bay. The two of them gently put her on the hospital bed. As they left, Colleen and Katherine thanked them.

"What seems to be the problem?" the nurse asked.

"I can't stop retching," Colleen said. "One minute I'm freezing, and the next minute I'm burning up."

A young, handsome doctor arrived and began asking Colleen questions. She began by saying she woke up with the chills, and then became very dizzy.

"What time was that?" he asked.

"I'm not sure. Maybe two or three in the morning."

"Well, it's five now," he said, glancing at his watch.

"Doctor," Katherine interrupted. "Excuse me."

"Who are you?"

"I'm Colleen's friend. I think she has food poisoning. We were at the Erie Hotel last night—"

"Oh, that's pretty unlikely," he interrupted. "I've lived here all my life and believe me, no one has contracted food poisoning from the Erie Hotel."

"I don't mean any disrespect, Sir, but to me she's exhibiting signs of acute food poisoning."

"And Ma'am, are you a doctor?"

"No, I'm not," Katherine said, surprised by his curtness.

"Then quite frankly, I think you should reserve judgment until you've graduated from medical school, and then we can have this conversation," the doctor said abruptly. He turned back to Colleen and said in a different tone of voice, "Your pupils are a little bit dilated, but that could be attributed to the excitement."

He began to examine Colleen. He looked in her mouth. He felt her stomach. "Does it hurt here?"

"Oh, no," Colleen said. "I think I'm going to get sick."

The nurse quickly handed Colleen a blue plastic bag.

"There's a stomach flu going around," the doctor explained. "I think you've caught it. I'm going to order a med to help you relax, and also something for your nausea. I'll have the nurse hook up an IV."

"But, why? I hate needles," Colleen said weakly.

"So, we can get some fluids in you right away. Also administering medicine via IV is the quickest way to stop you from throwing up. Okay," he said, smiling. "I'll check on you in a little while." He left the bay without looking at Katherine.

"Wow, I guess he bit my head off," Katherine whispered to the nurse.

The nurse shrugged and then said to Colleen, "I wouldn't worry, young lady. This bug usually doesn't last but forty-eight hours. You should be up and about soon enough."

"My plane back to New York leaves in a few days. I hope I'm able to make the flight."

"Let's not worry about it now," Katherine said.

The nurse finished her IV preparations and said to Katherine, "You might as well go home. She'll be here a minimum of four hours."

"No, I'm good. I'll stay with her."

"Katz, you don't have to," Colleen objected.

"Okay. I'll go home, feed the cats, and then come back. Not sure how, considering my car wouldn't start earlier. Nurse, is there a car service here? I need a lift back to Erie."

"Not that I know of, but if you want to wait a half hour, I can drive you home. I live in Erie, too."

"That would be great."

"Just sit in the waiting room and I'll come get you when my shift ends."

"Is that okay with you?" Katherine asked Colleen.

"Please check on me before you leave. I think I'll just go to sleep for a while."

"I'll let you rest."

Katherine made her way to the waiting area, picked a chair, and quickly nodded off. Within thirty minutes the nurse came in, tapped her on the shoulder and said she'd pull her car out front. Before Katherine left the hospital, she quickly checked on Colleen, who was fast asleep. Outside, the nurse pulled up and Katherine got in.

"Oh, I'm Mary Collins, by the way," the nurse said.

"I'm Katherine Kendall. I'm pleased to meet you."

"So where in Erie do you live?" she asked, driving out of the hospital's parking lot.

"512 Lincoln Street."

"512 Lincoln Street," Mary said excitedly. "Do you mean the Colfax mansion?"

"Yes, I just moved there on Sunday."

"Are you related to Mrs. Colfax?" Mary asked.

"She was my great aunt on my mother's side."

"I was so surprised to hear she had passed away," Mary said, stopping the car, then pulling out into the main highway.

"How do you mean?" Katherine asked curiously.

"She was such a spry old lady. I went to church with her. The last time I saw her, we were decorating tables for our annual bazaar. Your aunt bustled and fussed around and decorated more tables than I did, and I'm fifty years younger. A week later she was gone."

"That's odd," Katherine said suspiciously. "Someone told me a few days ago that my great aunt's health had deteriorated toward the end of her life, so much so that she was virtually housebound."

"Heavens, no," Mary said. "She was one spunky old gal."

They crossed the bridge and were heading down the hill to the town. They rode in silence the rest of the way.

* * * *

It was close to six in the morning when Katherine walked in the door. She went into the atrium, picked up the house phone, and dialed Mark Dunn. She thought he might recommend the name of a good mechanic with a nearby garage. When his answering machine picked up, she hung up, remembering that he was out-of-town attending a seminar. She found Cokey Cokenberger's business card in the pile of other cards on the curio cabinet and dialed his number. The phone rang two times and Katherine quickly put down the receiver, realizing that it was really early, and Cokey could still be sleeping. She'd have to be patient and call later.

But Colleen's mother would be up by now, she thought. She dialed Mrs. Murphy's number.

Colleen's mother answered on the first ring. "Good morning," she said cheerily.

"Mum. This is Katz," she said solemnly.

"How are you? Is everything okay?" Mrs. Murphy asked, beginning to sound worried.

"Colleen has the stomach flu. She's been retching since the middle of the night. I took her to the hospital."

"Oh, dear. What are they doing for her?"

"The doctor ordered something for the nausea."

"Are you with her now? Can I talk to her?"

Katherine quickly filled in Mrs. Murphy with the details and said she'd have Colleen call her as soon as she could.

"Thanks, Katz. You take care," Mrs. Murphy said, hanging up.

Katherine heard several raps on the side door and went to open it. Cokey Cokenberger stood outside.

"I hope you don't mind my bothering you so early, but I saw the lights on and hoped you would be up. I'm really anxious to finish the tuck-pointing job. I think if I start right away, I can be done by supper time."

"That sounds great. I'll go unlock the basement door."

"Meet ya there," he said.

Katherine walked to her office, unbolted the door to the basement, and moved slowly down the creaking wooden steps. She hated the eerie shadows cast on the stone walls by a single naked light bulb, and the musty smell of damp stone. She stopped for a minute and remembered how pitiful Vivian Marston looked, lying under a garbage bag with her foot hanging out.

There was a loud tap on the sunroom door. She hurried to unlock the door.

Cokey bounced in and said amicably, "The Weather Channel said we could get up to ten inches of snow."

"Snow—" she said absently, still thinking about the housekeeper.

"Yep. Wouldn't be winter without snow," he smirked.

Katherine feigned a smile and turned to go back upstairs. Then she remembered the car battery. "Cokey," she began. "Someone stole my car battery. I had an emergency early this morning. My friend got sick, and when I tried to take her to the hospital, I discovered my battery was missing."

"Who in the world would want to do a thing like that?" he asked, disgusted.

"Can you recommend a garage so I can call and get a battery delivered and installed today?"

"Pay no mind. I'll call myself. My cousin has a garage downtown. Hang on a minute," he said, getting his cell phone out of his back pocket. "Oh, Ben, Cokey here. Need a battery at the Colfax place. Really? That busy on a frozen day. Well, I'll let her know you can't come over until later this afternoon." Cokey disconnected the call. "Sorry," he said to Katherine. "He's tied up until later."

"I need to pick up my friend in a few hours."

"No problem. Just give me a holler and I'll take you," he said, turning to go in the next room.

"Thanks," she said, calling after him. She rushed upstairs and deliberately averted her gaze from the corner where Vivian Marston's body had been found.

Scout was behind the door at the top of the basement steps, chattering about something. "Get back, Scout," Katherine admonished. Scout ran to the center of the room, threw herself on the floor, and began rolling from side to side. "Waugh," she complained.

"Okay, I surrender," Katherine said. "I know you're hungry. I'm going to feed you now."

After feeding the cats on rose-patterned Haviland dishes, she went into the kitchen, poured water into the kettle, and set it down on the burner. As she struck a match and lit the gas jet, she heard the muffled sound of two people talking in the basement. At that moment, she didn't think anything of it, because Cokey was tuck-pointing the basement bricks. She thought one of his friends had joined him for a bit of conversation while he worked.

Scout trotted in and began nervously pacing back and forth in a figure-eight circle.

"What's the matter now?" Katherine said, petting the troubled cat.

"Waugh," Scout cried tensely. She ran a few steps and then turned around. "Waugh," she said, flinging her body against the stove.

"What is it?" Katherine asked, concerned. Scout ran out of the kitchen to the office door that led to the basement. Katherine hurried after her. Scout reached up with her brown paw and tapped the doorknob.

"You can't go down there," she said firmly, and then stopped. The conversation downstairs had become louder.

Scout pretzelled her lean body behind Katherine's legs, which prevented her from moving away from the door. The woman's voice in the basement was now sobbing.

"You led me to believe that if I had money, you'd divorce your wife," the voice cried.

"Where in the hell did you get that idea? I've told you from day one that I don't intend to divorce her," Cokey said.

"Don't you realize that as soon as my mother's estate is settled, I'll have tons of money? You could quit your job. We could build that log cabin we always talked about."

"Money doesn't mean a damned thing to me. I think you should take that money, finish school, and move as far away from here as possible."

"But I thought you loved me," the woman pleaded.

"Look, Patty, I don't mean to hurt your feelings, but I'm not interested. I'll never leave my wife and kids to be with you. You've got to understand that and leave me alone."

"Cokey, darling, you led me to believe that you would marry me," she choked.

"Patty, stop crying. She'll hear you."

"That witch," Patricia said. "Coming out here to claim what was rightfully my mother's inheritance."

"Shhh," Cokey warned. "I don't want you to talk bad about Ms. Kendall. I think she's a very nice lady."

Patricia continued to cry. Cokey said something to her that Katherine couldn't make out. The kettle began whistling on the stove, and Scout moved so Katherine could return to the next room. Katherine feared that the couple below could hear her footsteps on the creaking wood floor. She felt she had violated their privacy by eavesdropping. She had learned something about the handyman that she didn't care to know. He was the married man whom Vivian Marston had referred to.

Katherine changed her mind about the tea. She gazed out the kitchen window and watched Patricia Marston leave. She grabbed her cell phone and called the hospital to inquire about Colleen. The voice on the other end said that Colleen was doing much better and could be picked up any time after eight.

Katherine took a quick shower, dried her hair, and then thought how awkward it would be to ask Cokey for a lift to the hospital after overhearing his conversation. But it turned out easy. She was checking her email when there was a light rap on the office door. It was Cokey.

"Hey, I heard the click and clack of your keyboard. Want to go now?" he asked.

Katherine opened the door. "Yes, of course. I'll get my coat."

"I'll be in the truck," he said, leaving.

"Wait just a second," Katherine said. "I'm coming out the front door."

"I'll drive to the front and meet you there," he said.

Katherine hurried to find her coat, purse and house key. After she locked the front door, she trudged in the snow to the truck. She had trouble getting into Cokey's Dodge Ram.

"Use the running board," he said. "Take my hand. I'll pull you in."

She got in. "I really appreciate this."

"No problem."

He was clearly upset about something, she thought. He barely spoke on the way. When they got there, he said, "I'll just wait here."

Katherine entered the hospital and found her friend sitting up in a wheelchair. "Hey, how are you?"

"Ready to hit my bed," Colleen said. "But at least I'm not retching anymore."

The nurse suggested Katherine check Colleen out, so Katherine headed to the front desk. She signed a discharging patient form and then returned to Colleen, who had fallen asleep in the wheelchair. Katherine tapped her on the shoulder and said, "Hey, Missy, we've got to go now."

The nurse grabbed the handles and pushed Colleen out. As if on cue, Cokey pulled the truck to the front. He got out and helped Colleen inside; she sat in the middle. Katherine climbed in after Colleen. Cokey got in and fired up the engine. "Look at that snow," he observed, pulling out. "It's really coming down."

When they got to the house, Katherine noticed a car parked behind her disabled car and said to Cokey, "Yay! Your mechanic friend is here."

"No, that's not Ben's car," Cokey answered. "That's some kind of rental car. See the sticker on the back bumper. Plus, it's got Illinois plates. Know anyone from Illinois?"

"Not really. I don't see anyone sitting in it," Katherine said, getting out. "Well, it's snowing to beat the band. We'll figure it out later once I have Colleen upstairs."

"Can I help?" Cokey offered.

"No, we're good. Thanks," Colleen said.

"Listen, I have to get something at the hardware store. I'll be back in a minute. Can you unlock the basement door?"

"Sure," Katherine said. And then to Colleen, "Can you make it?"

Colleen slid off the truck seat. The two trudged through the snow, making their way to the front door.

"Let me get you to bed, and then I'm going to tell you something you'll not believe."

"Why wait? Tell me now," Colleen implored.

"Our Mr. Cokey had an affair with Patricia Marston."

"Oh, no way. What makes you think that?"

"Because of something I overheard this morning," Katherine said as she turned the key in the lock. As they mounted the stairs to the second floor, she filled in the details of the conversation.

"She has a lot of nerve setting foot in this house after she quit without notice. She has no business here."

Katherine nodded and said, "Oh, remember the cigarette lighter we found in Abby's stash in the chair lining? I'm pretty sure Patricia gave that to Cokey. Remember the inscription: *To Cokey with Love* with a letter scratched out? I think the letter was an initial, 'P' for Patricia."

Colleen's eyes widened. "You think? Where did she get the money for that? It looked expensive. How did he react when you gave it back to him?"

"I didn't. I can't find it. I think Abby took it again."

"The thief with bangs," Colleen mused. "Katz, here we are," Colleen said entering her bedroom. "I'm feeling really sleepy again."

"You get some rest. I'm going downstairs and try to solve the rental car mystery."

"Maybe in an hour or so could you bring me some tea?" Colleen asked, covering herself with a comforter.

"Will do. Hey, if you need anything, just call me on my cell. We'll pretend the house has an intercom system."

Katherine closed the door and walked down the hall. A very agitated Iris met her.

Iris hissed and ran down the stairs. She began to frantically paw on the pocket door that led to the dining room.

"What's wrong, sweet girl?" Katherine asked, following her. When she slid the pocket door open, she instantly knew something peculiar had taken place while she'd been away. The overhead cranberry glass chandelier was on and one of the drawers to the Eastlake hutch was partially open. She snatched Iris, who tried to get down, but Katherine held her tight. She ran to the powder room by her office and shut Iris inside. "I'll be right back."

Iris snarled.

Katherine walked into her office and was alarmed to see the basement door standing wide open. *The other cats are in the basement*, she realized with sudden panic. She flipped on the stairwell light and ran down the stairs two at a time. On the bottom landing, she stopped dead in her tracks. She distinctly heard Scout.

"Scout," she called. "Where are you?"

Scout's shrill Siamese cry echoed from the farthest recesses of the dimly lit basement. Katherine followed the sound. After a few steps, she squinted and saw Scout outside the turret room door, engaged in the same kind of Halloween cat dance she had performed around Vivian Marston's corpse several days before.

Katherine hesitated, not wanting to go any further. A strong sense that something wasn't right came over her. "Scout, come to me," she coaxed.

Scout bellowed a low, throaty growl and continued arching her back, hopping up and down, and salivating at the mouth like a rabid animal. The fur on the back of her neck was bristled, her ears were flattened, and her tail was bushed out all the way to its tip.

"Stop it. Come to me this instant," Katherine insisted.

Scout darted into the turret room.

Katherine chased after her, but hesitated outside the doorway, terrified of what she might find inside.

Another shriek from Scout forced her to react. She lunged into the room and tripped over a long, unyielding object on the floor. She rolled over on her side and stared directly into the face of a man. "No-o-o," she screamed, recognizing her former boyfriend.

In a bizarre gesture, someone had stuffed the gold cigarette lighter into Gary DeSutter's mouth. With trembling hands, Katherine stifled her sobs and tried to compose herself.

"Gary!" she shouted. "Gary!" She shook his shoulders. "Gary, wake up," she demanded. She felt his wrist for a pulse, but couldn't find one. She felt his neck, but there was no pulse there, either. There was a knife sticking out of his armpit; the blade deep inside.

It was then she noticed the blood—pools of blood— warm and sticky. She jumped up and slid in the blood as she fumbled to find the chain to the overhead light bulb. When she turned the light on, she screamed, "Abby, no," she cried. "Oh, no."

Abby lay on her side in the corner, motionless.

Cokey Cokenberger ran in. "What happened here?" he asked, shocked. "Who is this man?"

"He's dead. There's no pulse. Call 911. I have to take care of Abby."

"What's wrong with her? She's covered in blood." Cokey quickly examined the cat, then said, "I don't think this is her blood." He found his phone and called 911.

The 911 operator answered. Cokey recognized her voice as his niece. "Maureen, we've got a situation here at the Colfax house. I need Chief London over here ASAP. Somebody's been stabbed to death. And tell him to drive down the back alley, because the driveway is blocked with vehicles. Oh, and get a hold of Dr. Sonny. Tell him to stop

262

whatever he's doing and get over here pronto. Orvenia's cat has been injured."

"Right, got it," Maureen said, hanging up.

"They're on their way," Cokey said to Katherine, who had picked up Abby and was holding her in her arms.

"She's breathing, but her pupils are super-dilated," Katherine said in a trembling voice.

"Ah, I think she's in some sort of shock. You've got blood on you, too. Are you alright?"

"Yes, I'm fine."

"Is that the guy's rental car parked outside?" Cokey asked, gesturing to the body.

Katherine nodded. "And the story gets even richer. He's my ex-boyfriend, Gary, from New York. I don't know why he's here. I don't know how he knew where to find me. I don't have a clue what's going on."

They could hear the police sirens wailing in the distance.

"Cokey, please hold her," she said handing Abby to the handyman. "I have to get Scout out of here."

"Are you sure that's a good idea? The chief will be here any minute."

"I don't care," Katherine said, then thought, *I don't want the chief to see Scout at yet another crime scene. Gary's dead*, she sadly rationalized, *but my cat isn't.*

"Scout, baby, come to me? I'm going to take you upstairs," Katherine said as soothingly as possible.

"Waugh," Scout screeched.

Katherine cornered the terrified Siamese and grabbed her around the middle. Scout struggled desperately, but Katherine held on tight. She wrestled Scout out of the basement and up the stairs. She opened the powder room door and gingerly put Scout inside. Scout sneezed a couple of times and then went over to Iris. "Waugh," she said, collapsing next to her. Iris curled up her lips as if she'd smelled something disgusting, then began grooming Scout fastidiously with her pink tongue. Scout began to purr, so Katherine knew she could leave the two of them confined together without fear of Scout performing any more bizarre death dances.

Colleen heard the commotion and ran into the office. "What's going on? I heard you scream. Katz, you've got blood on you."

"Gary was murdered in the basement. And Abby's injured."

"Oh, for the love of God," Colleen said, collapsing in a chair. "I feel like I'm going to faint. This is unbelievable."

"The police are coming any minute. Have you seen Lilac?" Katherine asked hurriedly.

"No, why?"

"I can't find her, and I'm afraid she's running amok in the basement," Katherine said, at her wit's end.

"I'll look for her," Colleen said.

"Please go back to bed and stay there. I don't want you implicated in anything."

Katherine grabbed a sweater off the chair and rushed back down to the basement. She went to the sunroom door to open it for the police. She was startled to find the door to the outside ajar—a small pile of snow had blown in on the floor. *That's how the killer got in,* she thought. *And, Gary! Cokey must have forgotten to lock the door when he left, and the wind blew it open, but why didn't he close it when he came in?*

Chief London and Officer Glover drove up, with all lights flashing and tires crunching on the icy alley behind the house. They got out of their vehicle and did a brisk walk to the pink mansion. They rushed over and stepped down into the sunroom.

"Another body in the basement, Ms. Kendall?" the chief said irritably. "Want to show us where it is?"

"This way." Katherine motioned to the two officers, who followed her to the turret room in the farthest corner of the basement.

"What happened?" the chief asked Katherine. He adjusted his holster so he could crouch down and look at the body.

Katherine was about to hand the sweater to Cokey, but he'd already placed Abby in his winter jacket. "I got home a few minutes ago," she began, "I found my office basement door open, and came down here to investigate."

"Did you think you had another prowler?" the chief asked.

"Actually, I thought Cokey had returned from the hardware store and somehow got in because I hadn't had time to go down and unlock the door for him."

"Cokey, what's your part in this?"

"I'd just come back from Ed's store when I heard a scream. I ran back here and found Ms. Kendall tending an injured cat. This gentleman, I'm afraid, was lying dead on the floor."

"Ms. Kendall, do you know this man?"

"Yes," she answered sadly. "He must have rented a car and driven here to see me. We had broken up several months ago. I haven't spoken to him since I left Manhattan last Saturday."

"That's his rental car parked outside," Cokey added.

The chief asked Katherine, "You said you'd just got home. Where had you been?"

"My friend, Colleen, became ill last night. I rode in an ambulance to the hospital. She was admitted for several hours. I got a ride back to Erie. Then I asked Cokey to take me back to the hospital because she was being released. He drove me there, and then the three of us came back to the house. I brought Colleen inside and he went to the hardware store."

"Well, I know this man wasn't murdered while I was tuck-pointing earlier this morning," Cokey observed. "This had to have happened while I took Ms. Kendall to the hospital," he explained.

"And what time was that?" the chief asked.

"Oh, I think about eight o'clock."

"Has anyone else been in the house this morning?" the chief asked.

Katherine looked at Cokey curiously.

Cokey answered, looking down at the floor. "Patricia Marston was here, but only for a few minutes."

"The gal who works at the hotel? Vivian Marston's daughter? What did she want so early in the day?"

"Ah," Cokey said nervously. "She was looking for something she lost. She didn't say what it was."

"In the basement?" the chief asked incredulously.

"Well, she works for Ms. Kendall—"

"Not anymore," Katherine interrupted. "She quit yesterday."

"What was her job here?" the chief asked.

"Landscaping. Gardening," Cokey said. "In the summer she mowed the grass and tended to the flower gardens."

"Do you think she came back while you took Ms. Kendall to the hospital?"

"I don't know," Cokey said, shaking his head. "But she's been a loose cannon lately."

"And how is that?" the chief asked.

"It's a long story . . ." Cokey began.

"We'll talk about it later," the chief said. Then he looked at Officer Glover and said, "We've got us a homicide, Dan. Get the coroner over here. Get the State Police. We'll need a forensics team. And call in for Officer Silver to invite Patricia Marston to the station for a little chat. You know the drill."

"Yes, Sir," Officer Glover said, leaving the room.

Katherine took Abby from Cokey and cradled the cat in her arms. Abby moaned.

"The vet is on his way," Cokey said to the chief.

"I don't want the vet walking in here and disturbing the crime scene. Hand her to me. I'll have Officer Glover take her."

"Thanks," Katherine said, carefully handing Abby to the chief.

"I want you two," the chief said after he'd returned, "to walk around the edge of this room and wait for me in that room in the front." For the first time, the chief observed the blood on Katherine's jacket. "What's that?" he pointed.

"When I came in here, it was so dark. I didn't see Gary on the floor. I tripped over him. Can I wash this blood off me?"

"No," the chief barked. "We want to make sure your blood and DNA are not on the murder weapon. Do as I ask."

Cokey escorted Katherine out of the room.

"What happens now?" Katherine asked, sitting down on one of the wicker chairs.

"Well, I assume the chief will want a statement, and then the State Police will interview us."

Katherine fished out her cell phone and called Mark Dunn. She left an urgent voice mail. Then she texted Colleen, "Did you find her?" In a few seconds, the phone pinged. "No. Still looking," the screen indicated.

Katherine buried her head in her hands and sobbed. "Gary is dead and Lilac is missing."

"Is Lilac one of your cats?"

"Yes, and I can't go look for her."

"Do you think she got outside?"

"I'm not sure but she could have."

"I'll text my son and have him look for her. What color is she?"

"She looks like a Siamese but her mask and points are gray."

Cokey sent his son a text message with the information. "I wouldn't worry, Ms. Kendall. I bet Lilac is hiding somewhere in the house. She probably heard the commotion in the basement and then the police sirens. I'm bankin' she's not outside."

"Thanks," she said, then added, "Cokey, I heard your conversation with Patricia this morning."

"Damn, I was afraid of that. She just won't leave me alone. She's like a stalker. She follows me from job site to job site. She parks in front of my house and just sits there. I'm scared to death my wife will find out, which is why I haven't gone to court for a restraining order."

Officer Glover entered the house and said to Katherine, "Hey, Dr. Sonny just took your cat. You need to call him."

After she thanked him, Katherine quickly tapped in the vet's number and left her pertinent information with the front desk. When Officer Glover left the room, she said sternly to Cokey, "Do me a big favor? Don't ever let that woman in my house again, got it?"

"Got it," he said guiltily.

Chapter Ten

Katherine sat in the parlor, sipping a glass of wine, and thought about what a horrible day it had been. She was thankful that Colleen was okay, and was relieved that Lilac had been found. Last time she checked on Colleen, she was fast asleep, with Lilac curled up next to her.

Iris and Scout had joined Katherine and were sitting like bookends on the claw-footed sofa. Every once in a while, Scout would go to the large picture window and try to capture a snow flake, just like she'd done at the motel in Pennsylvania. *That seems like a century ago*, Katherine thought. She was having second thoughts about staying in Indiana. At this point, she didn't give a damn about the inheritance. She had her own money. But she did care about Abby, and didn't want to leave her. She was waiting for Mark Dunn, who had been delayed in the city because of the snowstorm.

Joining Scout at the picture window, she looked out onto the street. Eight inches of snow had piled up, and large, wet flakes continued to fall. A snow plow truck drove by with a Honda driving right behind it. Mark parked in front of the house, and then came up the sidewalk.

The loud clang of the doorbell sent Iris and Scout scurrying upstairs. Katherine rushed to open the door before Mark rang a second time.

"I left the seminar as soon as I could," Mark apologized. "I'm so sorry I didn't get your message until the noon break. I started back to Erie right away, but I had problems in Brownsburg," he said breathlessly.

"I'm just glad you're here and that you've arrived safely. Please come in," she said, moving away from the door. "Would you care for a glass of wine? It's a nice Merlot."

Mark took off his coat and casually laid it across a chair. He slipped off his boots and then walked into the parlor. "Yes, I'd love one. I-74 was a mess. I actually spun off the road. Fortunately, a tow truck was in the vicinity and pulled me out."

"Did it damage your car?" she asked, concerned.

"A little scrape on the back fender. It's fixable," he said.

"Oh, how scary," Katherine said. She poured him a glass and handed it to him. He took a long sip and then sat down.

Katherine began pacing the floor, wringing her hands.

"But that's nothing compared to what you went through," he said gently. "If you don't mind telling me, I'd like to know."

Katherine found a chair near the gas-jetted fireplace. She didn't answer right away.

Mark said, "I basically know the gist of it from talking to Chief London, but I want to hear it from you."

"Chief London? When did you speak to him?"

"I called him from the road. We talked for quite some time."

"I don't know where to begin. My mother used to say that I'd begin every story with what I had for breakfast, but I didn't have breakfast, so here it is in a nutshell. My nightmare began with Colleen getting sick. I tried to drive her to the hospital, but someone had stolen my car battery."

"Really?" he said. "That kind of stuff rarely happens in Erie."

"Well, it did. I didn't get a replacement until late this afternoon, and now with snow in the driveway, I can't get out anyway. Gary's rental car was processed by the State Police and then towed to an impound lot." She filled him in on the rest of the details of the day. "It was bad enough to find my ex-boyfriend dead on the basement floor, but poor little Abby was lying in the corner. I thought she was dead, too."

Mark commiserated, "That poor little cat."

"I thought she'd been stabbed also because she had a lot of blood on her, but now I realize it was Gary's blood."

"Did you know Gary was coming? I know that's a nosy, personal question."

"I don't have a clue why he would want to visit me, unless he wanted us to get back together."

"Well, I'm sure the police notified his next of kin."

"I called his sister Monica this afternoon. She'd already spoken to the Erie police and was making funeral arrangements. I'll need to fly out sometime early this week to attend his funeral."

"I can take care of your cats," Mark offered. "Just let me know."

"Thanks," she smiled.

"How's Colleen?"

"She's resting. She had quite an ordeal. When I brought her back from the hospital, she was supposed to go straight to bed, but she ended up searching the house for Lilac, who had gone missing."

As if on cue, Lilac walked into the room with a miniature stuffed bear in her mouth. She dropped it on Mark's shoe. "Me-yowl," she called loudly.

"Good girl," he said, petting Lilac's head.

Katherine continued to brief Mark on her eventful day. "I thought that Lilac had gotten out because the basement door to the outside was open. She could have easily slipped out, but later Colleen found her inside the lining under the seat of a wing back chair."

"You mean one of those chairs in the living room?" he asked.

"We call it "Abby's stash" because that's where we found a gold cigarette lighter belonging to Cokey."

"I don't think Cokey smokes. How did you know it was his?"

"From the inscription engraved on the side. I think Patricia Marston gave it to him."

"Patricia Marston? Why would she give him a lighter?" Mark asked, perplexed.

"This may surprise you, but Cokey and Patricia had an affair. I think it's over now."

"I'm intrigued. What are you *not* telling me?"

"This morning, before all hell broke loose, I heard Cokey and Patricia arguing in the basement. He said he didn't want to see her anymore."

"So, Cokey was working this morning? He must have let Patricia in."

She nodded. "Later Cokey took me to the hospital to pick up Colleen."

"Do you think Patricia stayed in the house after the argument?"

"I don't think so, because I saw her leave."

"Interesting," he said, taking another sip from his glass of wine.

"Then Cokey drove me to pick up Colleen. When we came back to the house, there was a car with a rental sticker parked behind my Toyota."

"Gary's, no doubt," Mark said. Lilac had curled up on his lap and was purring loudly.

Katherine nodded, then continued, "Cokey said he had to go buy something at the hardware store, so I took Colleen up to her room. When I came back downstairs, I thought I heard Scout in the basement. When I went to my office, much to my horror, the door to the basement was wide open, which was strange because I remembered specifically bolt-locking it."

"Was Scout down there?"

"I found Scout and Abby in that turret room on the east side of the house. It was so dark. I didn't see Gary, and I tripped over him. I must have screamed because Cokey ran in."

"Ah, I'm so sorry," Mark said.

"But I did something very stupid. I grabbed Scout and ran her up to the powder room. I must have gotten blood on my shoes because there were prints leading to the stairway."

"Why didn't you just call 911?" he asked.

"Because I wanted to get Scout out of harm's way so I could tend to Abby. She was lying on her side. It looked like she wasn't breathing."

"So, Cokey called 911?"

"Yes," she nodded. "When the chief arrived, he was his usual cranky self. He was taking pictures with his smartphone. One was of a bloody shoe print that was definitely not mine. I had my boots on, which has a smooth pattern on the underside. This print had grid marks, like a sneaker."

"Yes, the chief told me about that. That's a great piece of evidence."

"But even though he looked at my boots and could clearly see I didn't leave the print, he still made me give a statement."

"Standard procedure," Mark said. "And, Cokey had to give one, too, I presume."

"Yes. Cokey and I had to wait in the unheated sunroom for hours while the State Police processed the scene. We couldn't leave the room. Here Colleen is sick. Lilac is missing. Abby is at the vet. It was a nightmare. Oh, and the awful part of it was," she hesitated, then said. "I had blood all over my jacket—Gary's blood. The chief wouldn't let me change. Later, the State Police took my jacket into evidence."

"Did they fingerprint you?"

"Yes, I guess to eliminate me as a murder suspect."

"They were just doing their job, Katherine," Mark remarked. "You didn't touch the murder weapon, did you?"

"No," she said sadly, remembering the awful sight of Gary lying on the floor with a knife stuck in his side.

"So, I take it one of the officers took Abby to the vet?"

"Dr. Sonny came in person, I guess. I didn't see him."

Mark was silent for a moment, then said, "Well, here's what I think happened. I think Gary was at the wrong place at the wrong time. He came across this nut case in the basement. He was unarmed. The intruder, or whatever you want to call him, panicked and killed Gary."

"Until the police find the killer, I don't feel safe in this house. Even though you had Cokey change the locks, I feel the house isn't secure."

"Do you want me to stay the night until the locksmith comes tomorrow?"

"That's not a bad idea. I appreciate it." Katherine got up and poured the two of them more wine. "Mark, be honest with me, what kind of woman was my great aunt? Did she have enemies?"

"To be honest, she wasn't much liked in this town. She was an exceptionally smart woman, but very manipulative."

"How so?"

"She'd find out what people wanted and then promised that someday they'd have it."

"That sounds like something from *Faust*!"

"During this past year, Orvenia instructed me to revise her will three times. I have each of the revised wills digitally archived. The earlier versions were very complicated and listed numerous people. The one before the most current will designated Vivian Marston as the sole beneficiary."

"This I didn't know," Katherine said pensively. "If I just call it quits right now, what will happen?"

"You'll forfeit your right to inherit," Mark said in a matter-of-fact tone.

"But what happens to Abby?"

"Since Vivian Marston is dead, the inheritance and Abby will go to the next heir."

"And who, pray tell, is that?"

"Patricia Marston."

"Patricia Marston!" Katherine blurted. "She'll inherit Abby and everything else?"

"Orvenia was very clear in her instructions."

"Oh, Mark," Katherine said angrily. "This establishes motive. My gut instinct tells me Patricia has been doing all these terrible things from day one. This was her plan all along: to get rid of me somehow so she could inherit everything."

"Seriously, you don't think Patricia murdered Gary?" Mark asked. "You said yourself that you saw her leave the house."

"I don't know who killed Gary. Gary was a big guy. He worked out at the gym. I can't see a man or woman overpowering him. It just doesn't make any sense."

"You said earlier that Patricia was doing terrible things from day one. What did you mean?"

"For starters, she tried to scare me into going back to New York. She was in the house my first night here. Colleen thought she'd seen a ghost, but I'm sure it was Patricia, coming and going in the house, and using the back stairs to get out or hide."

"I checked the house that night, and I can assure you no one else was in the house," he said defensively.

Katherine continued, "She vandalized my room and Colleen's. And, when that didn't work, she tried to poison me."

"Poison you, how?"

"Hear me out. During my first trip to Indiana, I overheard a heated discussion between Mrs. Marston and her daughter," Katherine explained. "Vivian wanted Patricia to remove some kind of plant. She called it a weed. A Jim something. Well, I did an Internet search, and I think she was referring to Jimson Weed."

"Oh, yeah," Mark said. "You wanted me to look into it because you didn't want toxic plants around your cats. But when I checked later that day, most of the houseplants had been removed. I assumed Patricia had cleaned the area. But, I'm not familiar with Jimson Weed."

"Jimson Weed causes all sorts of problems. It can cause severe hallucinations. In other victims, symptoms can be falsely diagnosed as the flu. Colleen was diagnosed with the stomach flu. Like I said, I think Patricia has been trying to poison me from the get-go."

"How's that?" he asked.

"I think she minces Jimson seeds with poppy seeds. On my arrival, she'd baked poppy seed muffins."

"Ah, that's right," he remembered.

"The salad last night was meant for me. Colleen and I both swear Patricia put something in the poppy seed salad dressing."

"Did the ER doctor run a toxicology test?"

"No," she said. "He nearly bit my head off when I mentioned I thought Colleen had food poisoning. He was adamant that she had the flu."

"Unless you have a confession from Patricia or some hard evidence, that kind of accusation would be hard to prove."

"Yes, I know. It's circumstantial evidence. I watch a lot of crime dramas. But I also think she poisoned my great aunt and then killed her own mother."

"Orvenia Colfax was ninety-one years old. I'm not sure the State would want to pay for her to be exhumed in order to conduct a toxicology investigation," Mark said dismissively, then added, "However, if Jimson Weed causes delirium, that could explain how Vivian managed to walk over here from the nursing home. But the million-dollar question is, how did she get in the house?"

"This house is like Grand Central Station," Katherine said sarcastically. "Even with the doors locked, people get in, people get out. It's ridiculous." She rose from her chair and joined Mark on the sofa. "I think Patricia lured her mother to the basement. They had some kind of argument. And Vivian had a heart attack next to the water heater. I think Patricia was the one who covered her with a garbage bag. At least she cared enough about her to do that!"

"This is starting to gel. Patricia is an agronomy student. Of course, she'd know that the seeds were toxic and could kill."

"So, don't you think we should tell the police?"

"Hang on," he said, taking his Blackberry out of his shirt pocket. "I'll send the chief a text."

"You text the chief? Are you best friends or something?"

Mark was amused and said, "We're friends. We play golf together."

"Figures," Katherine said. "Everyone in this town is connected somehow."

"Speak of the devil," Mark said, putting down the phone. "The chief just pulled up outside."

Katherine looked out to see the chief's vehicle with its lights whirling. She moved to open the door. The chief came in and stamped his boots on the floor mat.

"Good evening, Ms. Kendall," he said, and then to Mark, "Hey, glad to see you made it."

"The roads were a glare of ice," Mark said.

"Yeah, I know. I just saw the vet in the ditch. I pulled over to see if I could help him, but he said he'd already called a tow truck. He said I needed to take something to you, Ms. Kendall."

Katherine looked confused. "And what was that?" she asked.

"I promised Dr. Sonny to make a delivery." He opened his jacket and pulled out Abby. "Chirp," the rusty-brown cat cried, squeezing her gold eyes adorably.

"Oh, my sweet little girl," Katherine said, forcing back a sob. She gathered the small bundle of fur in her arms and held her close. Lilac sauntered over and began me-yowling loudly. Katherine took Abby into the next room and sat down. Lilac jumped up and licked the ruddy cat on the nose.

The chief and Mark came into the room. Mark sat down, but the chief remained standing. "Ms. Kendall, as the second reason for my visit, I need to update you on the latest information regarding your intruder this morning."

"Won't you have a seat?" Katherine offered.

"No, thanks. I'll come right down to business. We have a suspect in custody. She's being held until her initial court appearance, when bail will be set or denied."

Mark and Katherine exchanged inquisitive glances.

"Patricia Marston confessed to killing Mr. DeSutter," the chief said.

Katherine gasped.

The chief continued, "She also confessed to trying to poison members of this household."

"What's she being charged with?" Mark asked.

The chief answered, "Criminal homicide. Murder, that is, along with various other charges."

"But why did she kill Gary?" Katherine asked.

"She confessed to wanting to murder you, Ms. Kendall. Judging by the rage I observed when I mentioned your name, I'd say you're one lucky young lady."

"But please, you didn't answer my question?"

"Here's the story as I see it," the chief explained. "Mr. DeSutter stayed at the Erie Hotel last night. This morning Ms. Marston was his server. They started chatting and he told her he was trying to win you back. Patricia thought Gary was a threat to her inheritance. She thought she had to get rid of him because you two might get married and she'd really have a challenge on her hands. She said she put some kind of poisonous mushroom in his omelet at the hotel this morning."

"But she stabbed him with a knife," Katherine said, surprised.

"I guess she didn't think the mushroom was working fast enough," the chief said cynically. "Okay, here's the bizarre part. Patricia assumed Mr. DeSutter would go back to his room and die at the hotel. But Mr.

DeSutter got in his rental car and drove over here. Patricia had already arrived; she somehow lured him into the basement. She confessed to wanting to murder Cokey, but when Mr. DeSutter startled her, she killed him instead. Her twisted plan was to kill your great aunt's cat, kill Cokey, and then you. That's it in a nutshell. No pun intended," the chief said, starting to leave.

"But wait, I think Patricia poisoned her mother and my great aunt as well," Katherine said, getting up. "When I first came out here, I overhead Vivian and Patricia arguing about a plant she was growing in the sunroom, some kind of plant called Jimson Weed. I told Mark I didn't want it in the house when I moved out here."

"That's good to know. I'll run it by the coroner. Ms. Kendall, Patricia confessed to a lot, but killing her mother or your great aunt was not one of these things."

"If Patricia didn't poison her mother, how did Vivian die?"

"Personally, I'd say she died from a heart attack."

Katherine looked askance, in disbelief. "And, as she lay dying, wedged between the wall and the water heater, she covered herself with a garbage bag."

"The State Police sent the bag to the crime lab where it'll be analyzed for fingerprints. I'm bankin' Patricia's prints will be on the bag. So . . . case closed," the chief said, tipping his hat. "I want to apologize to you, Ms.

Kendall. I'm truly sorry for the events of this past week, and hope that your stay here in the future will be free of any incidents."

"Thank you," Katherine said, still cradling Abby. "But what tipped you off that Patricia was the murderer?"

"The gold cigarette lighter stuck in Mr. DeSutter's mouth. When I reached the station to talk to her, I pulled the evidence bag with the lighter out of my jacket and showed it to her. At first, she went into such a rage about how much she hated Cokey and you, I had to cuff her to the chair. She then seemed to calm down and started crying. After that, she started talking. So, are we good here?" he asked.

"Yes," Katherine and Mark answered.

"Then good evening," he said, as he walked out the door.

Colleen hurried into the room, "What's going on? I saw the flashing lights and then got up to see what the heck was going on. What did the chief want?"

"Murder solved," Katherine said. "Patricia Marston confessed."

"Oh, the saints preserve us," Colleen said, finding the nearest chair to collapse in.

Mark looked at Katherine and said, "Do you still want to forfeit your inheritance?"

"No," Katherine said. "I'm going to stay."

"But I'm not," Colleen winked. "I have a flight out of Indy, and I certainly hope this weather lets up so I can go home."

"I feel both relief and sadness," Mark said, getting up. "Relief that we know who the killer is, but sadness that a woman as brilliant as Patricia could so mess up her life."

"Are you not staying?" Katherine asked, somewhat disappointed.

"No need to now. I'll call it an evening. Good night, Ladies," he said. "And that also includes you, Miss Abby and Lilac."

After Mark left, Colleen said, "Katz, I'm really going to miss you. But promise me you'll come out for St. Patrick's Day."

"Yes, I promise, but I'm definitely buying a new car. I don't think the Toyota would survive another trip," she laughed.

Scout and Iris marched into the room shoulder-to-shoulder. Judging by their demeanor, it looked like they had been up to something. "Waugh," Scout announced. She began doing figure eights in the middle of the room. Abby and Lilac jumped off Katherine's lap, which startled the Siamese. Scout's fur bristled out like a Halloween cat, and Iris growled. Then all four cats galloped out of the room, with Lilac in the lead.

"Off to the races," Colleen said.

"Waugh," Scout cried loudly from the back office.

"We'd better check it out," Katherine said. Colleen and Katherine made their way to the office to find Lilac proudly standing next to the computer monitor.

Colleen walked over for a closer look and said, "Katz, you'd better take a look at this."

Katherine glanced over and studied the web page. Then she said to the lilac-point Siamese. "Oh, no you didn't?"

On the monitor screen was the Facebook page of Patricia Marston. Lilac me-yowled guiltily and dashed out of the room with the other three at her heels.

Colleen said excitedly, "We've got to post this online. This is incredible! A cat who surfs the Web!"

"Oh, hold on there, Missy! Let's just wait until the cats set up their own Facebook pages, okay?" She brought her hand up and covered her mouth so Colleen wouldn't see the smirk on her face. "I'm thinking that all the cats had a paw in this. Now, let's call it a day," Katherine said, shutting down the computer.

"I vote for sleeping in tomorrow," Colleen said drowsily.

"I'm not getting up until the cows come home."

290

They both giggled and went upstairs with the cats close behind.

THE END

Dear Reader . . .

I love it when my readers write to me. If you'd like to email me about what you'd like to see in the next book, or just talk about your favorite scenes and characters, email me at: karenannegolden@gmail.com

Thank you so much for reading my book. I hope you enjoyed reading it as much as I did writing it. If you liked *"The Cats that Surfed the Web,"* I would be so thankful if you'd help others enjoy this book, too, by recommending it to your friends, family, and book clubs, and/or by writing a positive review on Amazon and/or Goodreads.

I love to post pictures of my cats on my Facebook pages, and would enjoy learning about your pets, as well.

https://www.facebook.com/karenannegolden

Amazon author page: http://tinyurl.com/mkmpg4d

Binge reading adds zero calories. The following pages describe my other books in the series. If you love mysteries with cats, don't miss these action-packed page turners. Available on Amazon. Kindle and paperback.

Thanks again.

Karen

The Cats that Chased the Storm

Book Two in *The Cats that . . .* Cozy Mystery series

It's early May in Erie, Indiana, and the weather has turned most foul. We find Katherine "Katz" Kendall, heiress to the Colfax fortune, living in a pink mansion, caring for her three Siamese and Abby the Abyssinian. Severe thunderstorms frighten the cats, but Scout is better than any weather app. A different storm is brewing, however, with a discovery that connects great-uncle William Colfax to the notorious gangster John Dillinger. Why is the Erie Historical Society so eager to get William's personal papers? Is the new man in Katherine's life a fortune hunter? Will Abra mysteriously reappear, and is Abby a magnet for danger?

A fast-paced whodunit, the second book in "The Cats that" series involves four extraordinary felines that help Katz unravel the mysteries in her life.

The Cats that Told a Fortune

Book Three in *The Cats that . . .* Cozy Mystery series

In the land of corn mazes and covered bridge festivals, a serial killer is on the loose. Autumn in Erie, Indiana means cool days of intrigue and subterfuge. Katherine "Katz" Kendall settles into her late great aunt's Victorian mansion with her five cats. A Halloween party at the mansion turns out to be more than Katz planned for. Meanwhile, she's teaching her first computer training class, and a serial killer is murdering young women. Along the way, Katz and her cats uncover important clues to the identity of the killer, and find out about Erie's local crime family . . . the hard way.

The Cats that Played the Market

Book Four in *The Cats that . . .* Cozy Mystery series

If you love mysteries with cats, don't miss this action-packed page turner. A blizzard blows into Indiana, bringing gifts, gala events, and a ghastly murder to heiress Katherine "Katz" Kendall. It's Katherine's birthday, and she gets more than she bargains for when someone evil from her past comes back to haunt her. After all hell breaks loose at the Erie Museum's opening, Katherine and her five cats unwittingly stumble upon clues that help solve a mystery. But has Scout lost her special abilities? Or will Katz find that another one of her amazing felines is a super-sleuth?

With the cats providing clues, it's up to Katherine and her friends to piece together the murderous puzzle . . . before the town goes bust!

The Cats that Watched the Woods

Book Five in *The Cats that . . .* Cozy Mystery series

What have the extraordinary cats of millionaire Katherine "Katz" Kendall surfed up now? "Idyllic vacation cabin by a pond stocked with catfish." It's July in Erie, Indiana, and steamy weather fuels the tension between Katz and her fiancé, Jake. Katz rents the cabin for a private getaway, though Siamese cats, Scout and Abra, demand to go along. How does a peaceful, serene setting go south in such a hurry? Is the terrifying man in the woods real, or is he the legendary ghost of Peace Lake? It's up to Katz and her cats to piece together the mysterious puzzle. The fifth book in the popular "The Cats that . . . Cozy Mystery" series is a suspenseful, thrilling ride that will keep you on the edge of your seat.

The Cats that Stalked a Ghost

Book Six in *The Cats that . . .* Cozy Mystery series

If you love mysteries with cats, get ready for a thrilling, action-packed read that will keep you guessing until the very end. While Katherine and Jake are tying the knot at her pink mansion, a teen ghost has other plans, which shake their Erie, Indiana town to its core. How does a beautiful September wedding end in mistaken identity . . . and murder? What does an abandoned insane asylum have to do with a spirit that is haunting Katz? Colleen, a paranormal investigator at night and student by day, shows Katz how to communicate with ghosts. An arsonist is torching historic properties. Will the mansion be his next target? Ex-con Stevie Sanders and the Siamese play their own stalking games, but for different reasons. It's up to Katz and her extraordinary felines to solve two mysteries: one hot, one cold. Seal-point Scout wants a new adventure fix, and litter-mate Abra fetches a major clue that puts an arsonist behind bars.

The Cats that Stole a Million

Book Seven in *The Cats that . . .* Cozy Mystery series

Millionaire Katherine, aka Katz, husband Jake and their seven cats return to the pink mansion after the explosion wreaked havoc several months earlier. Now the house has been restored, will it continue to be a murder magnet? Erie, Indiana is crime-free for the first time since heiress Katherine, aka Katz, and her cats moved into town. Everyone is at peace until domestic harmony is disrupted by an uninvited visitor from Brooklyn. Why is Katz's friend being tracked by a NYC mob? Meanwhile, ex-con Stevie Sanders wants to go clean, but ties to dear old Dad (Erie's notorious crime boss) keep pulling him back. Murder, lies, and a million-dollar theft have Katz and her seven extraordinary cats working on borrowed time to unravel a mystery.

The Cats that Broke the Spell

Book Eight in *The Cats that* . . . Cozy Mystery series

When a beautiful professor is accused of being a witch, she retreats to her cabin in the woods. Soon a man dressed like a scarecrow begins to stalk her, and vandals leave pentagrams at her front gate. The town of Erie, Indiana has never known a witch hunt, but after the first accusation, the news spreads like wildfire. "She stole another woman's husband, then murdered him," people raged in the local diner. "She uses her black cats to cast spells to do her evil deeds!" But what do the accusers really want? How is Erie's crime boss involved? In the meantime, while the pink mansion's attic is being remodeled, Katz, Jake and their seven felines move out to a rural farmhouse, which is next door to the "witch." They find themselves drawn into a deadly conflict on several fronts. It's up to Katz and her seven extraordinary cats to unravel the tangle of lies before mass hysteria wrecks the town. Murder, mayhem, and a cold case make this book a thrilling, action-packed read that will keep you guessing until the very end.

The Cats that Stopped the Magic

Book Nine in *The Cats that . . .* Cozy Mystery series

This classic whodunit boasts a new cast of characters: a self-centered magician, a compulsive gambler, a sweet cat wrangler and her grandmother, a caring nurse, and a wealthy couple. How are their lives intertwined with a show cat named Abra? In 2009, two Siamese cats performed in Magic Harry's Hocus-Pocus show, in front of hundreds of devoted fans. But their lives were far from magical, and their careers were cut short when Abra was stolen backstage after a performance. Why did the magician increase the insurance on Abra days before she disappeared? Was Abra stolen and sold on the black market? Or did anonymous cat-lovers rescue her from a life-threatening situation? A wealthy tycoon wants a Siamese cat with a specific look for his dying wife. Why? Four years later, Abra ends up in an animal shelter. Where had she been during this time? Back in Erie, Indiana, Katherine and Jake work on borrowed time to piece the puzzle together before Magic Harry tries to take Abra away from them.

The Cats that Walked the Haunted Beach

Book Ten in *The Cats that . . .* Cozy Mystery series

This fast-paced mystery is chock-full of coincidences and bizarre twists. When Colleen and Daryl get together to plan their wedding, they can't agree on anything. Colleen is at her wits' end. Best friend Katherine votes for a time-out and proposes a girls' retreat to a town named Seagull, which borders Lake Michigan and the famous Indiana dunes. Mum is adamant they stay in a rented cabin right on the beach. Against Katz's better judgment, she agrees with Mum's plan — only on one condition: she's bringing Scout and Abra, who become very upset when she's away from them. With the Siamese in tow, Katherine and Colleen head to the dunes to find that Mum's weekend retreat is far from ideal. The first night, they have a paranormal experience and learn that a ghost walks the beach when someone is going to be murdered. Meanwhile, ex-con Stevie has a date with a woman he met online. But this news doesn't prevent the town gossips from spreading a rumor that he's having an affair with a married woman. How does Abra finding a wallet lead to a mix-up with dangerous consequences? It's up to Katz and her extraordinary cats to unravel a deadly plot that ends in murder.

Acknowledgements

I wish to thank my husband, Jeff Dible, who painstakingly edited the first draft and enthusiastically supported this project.

My appreciation also goes to my sister, Linda Golden, who read the novel and offered suggestions on how to make it better. And I thank Megan Golden, Melissa McGee and Bryan Putnam for their advice and support.

Thank you, Vicki Braun, my editor and Christy Carlyle, my book cover designer. It's been my pleasure to work with the two of you.

Thanks to my loyal readers, my family, and friends. The Cats that . . . Cozy Mystery series would never be without the input from my furry friends.

Made in United States
North Haven, CT
21 December 2021